THE POLITICALLY INCORRECT MAX TROTTER

Roger Quinn

Expose Crime Mystery Press

Cover design by: pro_ebookcovers
Cover photograph by: Leonard Di Gregorio
Library of Congress Control Number: 2018675309
Printed in the United States of America

DEDICATION

Ula
2008-2022

FAIRDEN, SOUTH CAROLINA

ACKNOWLEDGMENTS

I owe a deep sense of gratitude to my editors and friends who contributed their time and talent to *The Politically Incorrect Max Trotter.*

Leonard Di Gregorio, development editor, for helping me put the pieces together.

Martin Turnauer critiqued the manuscript, summarized key points and made suggestions for the book.

Caroline "Tinker" Frazier, copy editor. Tinker meticulously read the manuscript and noted the spelling, punctuation, grammar mistakes, and style for the book's genre. Thank you for your encouragement.

Please attribute errors or omissions to me.

PROLOGUE

My name is Matt Nagle. I am the editor and narrator of the memoir you are about to read. *The Politically Incorrect Max Trotter* is the story of a septuagenarian, in fear of losing self-worth in a culture that glorifies youth and wealth.

Energized by sexual tension, *The Politically Incorrect Max Trotter* is a light-hearted, self-effacing, faux memoir. Along a road less traveled, Max Trotter discovers that living a life of postponed dreams while at the same time doing what others expect of him can be complicated. Life is complex, as is assembling an over-the-hill garage band, a metaphor for Max's obscure illusion of reality.

Cultures create words to express what is valued and privileged in a rapidly changing society. Many Americans are reluctant to discuss controversial topics in fear of being labeled un-American by those on the right and the left of so-called political correctness. Candid conversations are vanishing. Ostracism has powerful negative outcomes.

These are perilous days for writers. They walk a fine line between managing their reputations and the ever-expanding list of "cancel culture" taboos. As someone wrote, "Words are powerful, and perceptions become a reality." The term "woke" has become weaponized.

From a practical vantage, I encouraged Max to edit his memoir in such a way that it avoids risking the amity of esoteric readers. In the end, Max and I concluded that countless revisions would not evade irate criticism. People have lost their sense of humor.

Some readers may find this faux memoir controversial or offensive. Others will discover some excellent stuff.

Please keep in mind that The Politically Incorrect Max Trotter contains mature sexual content that may not be appropriate for all adult readers.

And now, without further ado, join Max Trotter and his ever-decreasing, but loyal circle of friends as they unleash your imagination.

❋ ❋ ❋

"It doesn't interest me how old you are. I want to know if you will risk looking like a fool – for love, your dreams, and the adventure of being alive."

Oriah Mountain Dreamer.

CHAPTER ONE

"Welcome to Jugzjava.com"

Hello, and welcome to Jugzjava.com. It's quiet for this time of day. You arrived just in time. Thirty minutes from now, the regulars will arrive with their laptops, tablets, and notebooks.

Jugzjava.com, the locals call it Jugz, gets busy and crowded at times. I've seen days when a line of customers stretched out the door. Jugz is a local café with a personal touch. Most of all, this café offers a unique Southern hospitality.

My name is Matt Nagle. I'm a customer and not a "barista." I'm part-owner of Emma's Bookstore, across from Fairden's Municipal Building on Front Street. Please stop and browse our shelves and displays. We encourage and feature local authors. But I'm not here to promote Emma's Bookstore; that's another story.

Several months ago, Max Trotter, a friend and frequent visitor to Emma's Bookstore, asked me to edit his short stories and anecdotes. At first, I declined.

A few weeks later, Max asked again, and I agreed. He returned with a box filled with folders and dropped it on the front counter. "Here!" Then with a theatrical flourish, he left.

❋ ❋ ❋

That evening I rummaged through the cardboard box

and read notes from a trip Max and his entourage had taken to Cuba a few years back. The following day, I called Max and asked him to meet me at Emma's Bookstore.

"I'll be right over."

Within minutes Max arrived wearing a raincoat over his pajamas.

"Max, I'm an author not a playwright. The few pieces I read last evening lend themselves to a three-act play."

"Wrong! Matt, please help me edit my collection. I'll reimburse you for the time. Make it an 'as told to' piece."

"Max, I write mystery novels with a touch of romance. This is your book. I'm not a ghostwriter. I'll give it a shot. You need a professional editor."

"You agreed to edit my work, Matt."

"And I will. I'm offering you a few alternatives before we get up to our ears in elephants. How about a musical? I'm not kidding. I've got it. *Max Trotter and The Over-The-Hill Garage Band* could be a musical production."

"Odd you mention that, Matt. I put the kibosh on the idea. Let's get back to the stories I left with you. What about the title?"

"That's up to you."

"There was a time when I was mesmerized by an international coffee brand that I hesitate to mention here," Max replied.

"Therein lies the problem. Most of your stories originated over a cup of coffee in a café you cannot or will not identify. Your reader needs to relate."

"You mean like *Cheers*?"

"Exactly. Imagine your characters sitting around a neighborhood café and sharing their woes."

"I suppose that might work." Max scratched his head, a sure sign he was drifting to the recesses of his mind.

"Hell. Change the name." Max turned, clasped his hands behind his back, and paced the store.

"To what?" I asked.

Max abruptly stopped pacing. "I have it. You're right. Keep the scenes but change the name of the café. Elmo French recently sold his beauty salon and opened Jugz. That's it. Move the settings to Elmo's place. Elmo French can use the publicity."

"We need Elmo's permission."

"I'll get it. This story demands a café."

"Max, come clean. Did you set the undisclosed cafés' locations as waypoints on your GPS when you traveled?"

"Exactly. It's a franchise, Matt."

"In China, too?"

"Yes. Years ago, I couldn't locate one in Italy. They've got one now. I did most of my research along the road."

"How?"

"A piece of cake. I carried my iPad or a notebook, picked a table where the acoustics suited my research, and everything else fell into place."

"Max, are you telling me you eavesdropped on conversations?"

"Correctomundo," Max replied with a huge grin.

"And that's why you have a folder marked Walmart?"

"Oh my god, Matt. That's the place to find interesting characters for any novel. The people I meet in Walmart fit right into your stories about Deepmarsh Village. There are a million stories in a naked Walmart."

"Max, the line goes, 'There are a million stories in the naked city.'"

"Matt, have you ever sat on a bench by the Walmart Greeter and people-watched?"

"No. Besides, Walmart replaced greeters with security guards."

"Doesn't matter. Sit on the bench. Check out the shoppers' shoes. Talk about 'soul-bearing.' A person's shoes give you a glimpse into their life story. Matt, your characters need more authenticity."

"Max, I've read a few of your anecdotes. They are

appalling. You enjoy character assassination. A gentleman never reveals his conquests."

"Nonsense. It's lighthearted. So what if I poke fun at a few people." Max raised his hands and shrugged.

"I'm warning you Max. These short stories could make you out to be a misogynist."

"Surely you are joking. I love women, Matt."

"In some circles your innuendos are offensive."

"That's old school, Matt. Readers demand stark-naked truth. Sex, and tell-all memoirs sell. Are you going 'woke' on me? Corruption, debauchery, and outrage are the American motivators. It's an excuse for woke anger."

"Woke? Don't play that card, Max. Coming from you, the term 'woke' flabbergasts me. Granted your stories are funny, but they are way out of line. Don't write because you think it will sell."

"Hold your horses, Matt. Your attitude toward writing is the reason your books don't sell. I've heard that you start writing at four in the morning. My god, how do you take a 'wiz' brush your teeth or make a cup of coffee at that time in the morning? Get a life."

Max's comment stopped me in in my tracks. "That hurt," I said.

"I've read your novels, Matt. Boring! Even your latest novel, *Brandi Barton*, doesn't go far enough. You need help with your sex scenes. Was the real-life Brandi open to *anything*? Hot damn, a man could spend a lifetime with a woman like that."

"It's a novel, Max."

"Sure, have it your way, you rascal. My book isn't a novel, Matt. It's a faux memoir." Max smiled. "I love women."

"Hold on. It's all about your age, Max. Current trends reveal women find older males sexually undesirable."

"You are too conventional, Matt. Readers demand sexual tension and feelings of arousal. Romance novels sell because readers want a happy ending." Max let out a low-pitched purr and growled. "Cougars don't roar like lions. They scream just before they pounce." Max raised his hand and pretended to claw Matt.

"Are you saying women are drawn to wealth, regardless of a man's age or physical appearance?"

"Get with it Matt. Cancel *The New York Times*. Get *Cosmopolitan Magazine*. *Cosmo's* the bible when it comes to great sex. Matt you better start reading romance novels. Sex, Matt. I'm warning you. Don't go woke on me."

"No! Max, your anecdotes are politically incorrect. Be careful. You'll get yourself in deep shit. Yesterday, I read that many of the classics are being updated to accommodate socially acceptable norms."

"No one would dare touch Ian Fleming's James Bond books."

"Yes sir. The original versions will be purged. No more 'fat,' and 'ugly.' 'Obey,' is definitely outlawed."

"Did the book inquisitors make those decisions, too?"

"Not sure. I'll leave that up to you to decide."

"In other words, *Naked Lunch* is a goner. Will we kiss Pussy Galore goodbye, too?"

"I think she's dead and buried, Max."

"But the classics were written within the context of their time, Matt. Is Ted Turner behind this? It's rumored that years ago he colorized movie classics and locked the black and white originals in a secret basement vault."

I shrugged. "Max I have no idea. There are only so many books a library can shelve. Perhaps the originals will be banned or burned along with the 1,500 now on the chopping block."

"But why, Matt?"

"It may have something to do with the reading level of the American public. It dropped from eighth grade to seventh. Americans want - no they demand - their books and movies to have happy endings. I guess it is only fair. They sense that something is not right. I try not to jump to conclusions about the cause of the malaise. Prurience, Max. It is an opioid, a fantasy outlet from a complex world."

"Don't you enjoy a happy ending, Matt?"

"Max, I mean the reading and viewing public want books and movies to have a positive outcome."

"You mean if it doesn't have a happy ending the book is banned and folks petition to close the movie theater?"

"Something like that. It boils down to morality, Max. I recall someone saying that most folks want to be morally ethical except when they can't - like on their taxes."

Max scratched his head, turned and disappeared into the row of shelves on the far end of the store.

❋ ❋ ❋

Minutes passed. Max's eyes fixed on the ceiling as though the sky was falling and sanity had flown the coop.

"Ah hah. I've go it. Matt, you're inspirational."

"Me? All I said is your anecdotes are sexist and socially and politically incorrect."

"Exactly. It's all about sex. That's the crux of today's cultural divide. All this time I thought the divide was over woke gender, cancel culture, and public shaming."

"Sex?" I frowned. "Max, that's a reach."

"And my readers will love it. Matt, you feel my stories are politically incorrect."

I nodded in agreement.

"Fantastic. And make sure you purge any hint of political correctness or socially redeeming value."

"*The Politically Incorrect Max Trotter*. The title fits the bill."

"Max, your readers will still recognize Dawn and Deidre Skipper, the Double D's."

"So be it. The precocious twins aren't a myth. It isn't an exaggeration that they are a Fariden legend for wearing more jewelry than clothes. Golfers are drawn to Fairden in hopes of catching a glimpse of the twins."

"I recall the grand opening of Emma's Bookstore. Elmo French encouraged Dawn and Deidre to show up in scanty two-piece outfits," I replied.

"It was a damn good publicity stunt, Matt. Elmo wanted folks to know that Jugz was coming to town. The mayor called Elmo a marketing genius."

"The mayor is a crook and serving time. Best you avoid his name," I replied.

"Great idea. I know that Elmo slept with the mayor's wife," Max insisted.

"There you go. Your revelation is a perfect illustration. That's character assassination. Max, we live in a world divided by politicians and their rapidly expanding lexicon of 'situationally-correct' words. It's tough speaking with a person without offending them somehow."

"Take it from me Matt, inspiring contempt and arousing suspicion earns big salaries these days. And that's good enough for me. I want to sell books."

"Maybe for you. But what about your reputation?" I asked.

"Matt, you are no Hemingway. Take it from me, if you want to be a successful writer, forget your reputation. You can't manage both at the same time."

"And the Skipper sisters?" I asked. "We must safeguard their reputations."

"Relax, Matt. The book is based on my opinions, not fact. Nevertheless, a name change can't disguise the twins. They are an unforgettable pair."

"One needs some degree of sensitivity," I insisted.

Max stifled a smirk. "I'll convince the Skippers to sign a nondisclosure agreement in return for an acknowledgment."

Max pointed to a manila folder next to the register. "Your contract is in there. Now let's get to work."

"Max, a writer needs to do research. I need to interview

your friends."

"You're free to tag along. That box contains a hell of a lot of conversations." Max hugged the box as though he was protecting national secrets minus redactions.

Just then Sandra, my business partner walked through the door.

Max was becoming so excited that he was shouting.

"A lot of hanky-panky in this box, Matt. I'm leaving it here. Guard it with your life. Any murders or embarrasing redaction failures will be on your conscience. Embellish and fabricate, but only lie when you must."

A dismayed Sandra turned and looked at Matt. "What the hell is wrong with Max?"

"I don't know."

Max walked to the magazine rack, grabbed a copy of *Cosmopolitan Magazine,* waved, and hiked out.

"He's got some balls taking that magazine without paying," Sandra complained.

"Oh, that's just Max," I'm trying to defuse the tension.

"Max's brain must work like a squirrel caught in traffic." Sandra could be sharp tongued.

I found a few photos among Max's files. Peculiar how all the folks in the snapshots had their backs to the camera.

"Wow. That reminds me of Mr. Wilson, Tim's almost faceless neighbor on Home Improvement," said Sandra. "Hey, don't include snapshots."

"Great idea," I replied. "I'll leave it to the reader to create a mental image of Max and his friends."

CHAPTER TWO

"Fairden, South Carolina."

Hello again. It's me, Matt, your narrator. Welcome to Jugz. Designed with a delightful architectural twist, the proprietor, Elmo French insisted that the café blend with Fairden's traditional local flavor.

Fairden found its roots in British history, but prided its Irish resilience. Fairden has the ability to survive and thrive, no matter the conditions. The mayor boasted that "Fairden has the biggest St. Patrick's Day parade north of Savannah."

The glass-domed atrium and full-service patio are perfect for watching fishing boats returning from downriver or a yacht hoisting sail as it departs the marina. I enjoy the evening river breeze after the rain. The golden light across the sky promises tomorrow will be a great day. Jugz is the ideal place to gaze at the opposite shore and daydream and perhaps fall in love.

The location has one drawback. The drive-thru window. On a foggy evening, an inattentive driver could accidentally take a right turn rather than a left and exit via the boat ramp.

Unlike many coffee houses, Jugz offers local and regional newspapers and magazines that still survive.

My favorite is *The River County Gazette.* There's free internet, too. After all, what would a cup of java be without a good read? Elmo French offers a low-acid blend – "The Elmo French Blend."

✽ ✽ ✽

You're just in time. Four of my favorite people, Max Trotter, Elmo French, and his companions, Dawn and Deidre, the Skipper twins, have arrived. When it comes to blowin' up a storm, the pretty-as-peaches twins can sure stir a man's testosterone.

Incidentally, one could never tell that Elmo French owns Jugz. Don't be fooled. He's a hawk when it comes to a buck.

Elmo's estranged wife, Silvia, managed Jugz until she ran off to India with her guru. But I'm getting ahead of the story.

Please take a few minutes to relax and enjoy this adventure. Max Trotter's saga is an experience to be savored one cup at a time. Again, my name is Matt.

✽ ✽ ✽

Jugzjava
"Lip Smackin and Thirst Quenchin."
Pick the size that suits your taste.
The Teaser – 8 oz. jug
The Sassy – 12 oz. jug
The Naughty –16 oz. jug

CHAPTER THREE

"Mother always preferred Howard Johnson's Restaurants."

"**G**ood evening ladies and gentlemen. Thanks for visiting Jugzjava.com. My name is Elmo French, the proprietor. We appreciate your patronage. Jugz is my brainchild. Rest assured, at Jugz, you are our priority. Great java, a casual atmosphere, and, most of all, clean restrooms.

I looked around expecting to find a group of tourists standing behind us. But, it was just the four of us.

Elmo continued. "Please take a deep breath. Enjoy the tantalizing aromas of our premium coffees. I've inherited my mother's acute sense of smell. My olfactory sense conjures memories. Forget the nonsense that low olfactory acuity portends a curtailed lifespan. Don't panic. A bad cold, allergies, and sinus problems can all affect your sense of smell."

"Allow me to share a poignant memory. When I was a child mother always preferred Howard Johnson's Restaurants," Elmo continued.

"Why?" I asked.

"Clean restrooms. Mother walked out of numerous restaurants with fancy facades because of a stinking, messy bathroom. Granted, she only checked the ladies' facility. Once the toilet seats passed inspection, it was safe to dine. Mother's wave and smile signaled the bathroom was clean and smelled clean, too. The last I heard, only one Howard Johnson's survives. Without saying, Jugz is carrying on their proud tradition. We take pride in being ADA compliant."

Then Max added, "Some odors are unforgettable," said Max. Until then, Max had been curiously quiet as were Elmo and the Skippers.

"Blindfolded, I can tell when I am in a nursing home. No amount of carpet shampooing will disguise that odor," remarked Dawn Skipper.

"When were you in a nursing home, you dummy?" asked the antagonistic Deidre Skipper.

Those two are always at each other's throat.

"Ladies please. Allow me to finish," Elmo scolded.

"Believe me. One visit to our restrooms and you'll be captivated," Elmo said with pride.

I was becoming a bit unsettled by Elmo's fixation with restrooms, so I gave him a signal to tie things up.

"Matt just signaled that I'm out of time," Elmo remarked. "Please stop at our gift shop and sample our fragrant candles. If you enjoy the aromas, you'll love our take-home assortment. And again, thank you for your patronage."

Elmo hopped off the platform and asked. "Well, Matt, how did I do?"

"Great job, Elmo. It was a touching piece of nostalgia. One suggestion," I said pointing to my iPhone screen. "You addressed our group as ladies and gentlemen. The guide on my phone suggests 'ladies' has negative gendered connotations. The guide recommends one might use the word 'women" instead. Better yet, the inclusive way to address a group might include 'y'all,' 'folks,' and 'people.'"

Not to put a damper on Elmo's ADA compliance I suggested he update his restroom signs. "Elmo, I might be wrong but your bathrooms don't comply with ADA standards."

"What? I can't say ladies? This whole politically correct thing is driving me crazy," Elmo replied.

I frowned and said, "Sorry Elmo. The word 'crazy' is a no-no, too."

"Like hell, Matt. I'd like to see someboday stop Willie Nelson. They'd be crazy for trying."

Then Dawn intervened. "Oh Daddy, don't be upset. What a great opportunity for a startup a company that produces a real-time politically correct and socially acceptable pocket translator."

"And how would that work?" grumbled Elmo.

"I have it," said an enthusiastic Max. "You say 'Good morning, assholes.' The translator regurgitates, 'Hi folks. Glad to see you.'"

"By god, Dawn, you and Max, hit the nail on the head. A real time translator address the the woke market gap. I could manufacture them three colors, red, blue and purple. Can you imagine the demand?"

❋ ❋ ❋

"Life is better with clean hands."
cdc.gov/handwashing.

Inclusive Restroom Sign
"Please Wash Your Hands."
Bigfoot Alien Sign
Found on Amazon.com

Jugzjava.com's full-service patio is the ideal setting to watch fishing boats returning from downriver or a yacht hoisting sail as it departs the marina.

CHAPTER FOUR

"The Politically Incorrect Bathroom Review."

After listening to Elmo French's childhood recollections of Howard Johnson's bathrooms, I feared toilets. I had nightmares about restaurant employees failing to wash their hands.

Germs preoccupied me. I couldn't chew on a pencil eraser without feeling nauseous. Now, I was about to be confronted by another ordeal.

Max Trotter caught me waiting for my Sassy and waved for me to join him.

"Here, take these, Matt." Max shuffled a stack of post cards and handed me a pile.

"What's this, Max?"

"I'm compiling data for *The Ultimate Bathroom Review*, Elmo's idea for a phone app."

"Can't you limit it to restaurants?"

"No. The health department places too much emphasis on kitchen cleanliness when it all begins with hand washing and toilet etiquette."

"I'll bet the Skipper sisters are behind this. They wallow in get rich schemes."

"Precisely."

"Max, I don't want to do this."

"I need your help, Matt."

"Then what?"

"Simple. Rate the bathroom one to five. A five earns five toilet seats for cleanliness."

"And the postcards?"

"Just drop them in a mailbox."

I glanced at the address on the postcard. "Max, who is L.L.C. Greedin?"

"L.L.C. is Elmo's attorney. He'll have one of his subcontractors inspect the location and then file a law suit. Elmo and L.L..C. worked a deal on splitting the settlements."

"Stop! Max, the plan sounds like frivolous litigation to me."

"Seems like everyone is litigating something these days, Matt. So, why not bathrooms?"

"Max, why do you let Elmo take advantage of you?"

"I'm a pleaser. Even the twins intimidate me. I'm afraid Elmo will call me woke," Max replied.

"Woke?" I frowned. "Now woke means to shut up?Elmo abandoned you to do the hump work. I've heard enough."
I placed the postcards on the table. "Max, this game plan doesn't work for me."

❈ ❈ ❈

"I used to spend so much time reacting and responding to everyone else that my life had no direction."
Melody Beattie

CHAPTER FIVE

"Duck and Cover."

Max Trotter's life was impacted by living his formative years in a funeral home.

A neatly mowed lawn and freshly painted trim often hide a multitude of secrets. Serenity Funeral Home proved no exception.

The outcome? Max Trotter lived in a world of illusion and magical causality. I recall one evening listening to one of Max's childhood stories.

"Matt, I discovered Santa was a myth when I was six. I was twelve when I stopped believing in the Easter Bunny. My imaginary friends helped displace the eerie silence of bodies in the basement mortuary. The incessant wailing of mourners in the Memories Room gave me the creeps. Imaginary friends and magical causality worked just fine for me."

I watched Max's eyes lower and move toward the right as though he was digging into his past and reliving the moment.

"My Uncle John posted slogans. 'Life can change in an instant' was my favorite since I found it to be true for the folks in the basement. God bless their hearts."

"Love songs permeated my life," Max confessed. But I recall one daunting slogan from elementary school- 'Duck and Cover.' It weaseled its way into my subconscious after listening to the news."

"Hey, I remember that one. We had a 'Duck and Cover' song, too. On a signal from our third-grade teacher, the class would shelter under our desks and turn away from the windows. I never asked, nor did our teacher explain, the game's significance or why she remained standing during the drill. I'll never forget the frog clicker. Two clicks - get under your desk. Three clicks - all clear."

"You know Matt, that bothered me, too. My dad told me folks thought the Russians were going to drop the big one."

"A bomb?" I asked. "My father, a man of few words, simply nodded and scowled. The rest I pieced together from television and playing war in an empty lot after school." Max began pacing the room as though he was looking for a table for shelter.

"For a while I feared the Russians might drop a bomb on my town," I added. "But 'Duck and Cover' was a bunch of crap," I told my friends. "They scoffed. And so, like you Max, I stopped believing in 'Duck and Cover."

"Matt, I pieced together my own rationale. The damn Russians were the culprits. It all made sense. I grasped the warnings. I felt powerless. And with all this current war talk I feel things are out of control. It's all coming back now."

"Matt, life seems more complex than when we were in elementary school. Still, when I was a kid, I never imagined an active shooter invading my school with an automatic rifle or handgun and randomly killing my teachers and classmates."

"Yes, Max, that is frightening. Duck and over seems pitiful compared with *Getout*, *Keep out*, and *Hide out,* children must practice as part of the new normal."

"It was so much simpler back when I was a kid. And I no longer have dad to help me figure it out."

Max's eyes began to glaze over, again, a sign he was drifting back to a safer, simpler place in time. "Max, are you okay?"

"Sure, Matt." Max shook his head to get rid of the cobwebs."When I was a kid, I would wish bad things would disappear. Most of the time that worked. I've lost the magic. I remember another one of my Uncle John's slogans."

"What's that one?" I asked.

"You can't save your ass and your face at the same time."

"Welcome to the real world, Max."

"I guess so, Matt."

"It was the best of times, it was the worst of times, it was the age of wisdom, it was the age of foolishness..."

Charles Dickens, A Tale of Two Cities

CHAPTER SIX

"Max Trotter's Hometown"

A nd now, with limited fanfare, it's time to present Max Trotter's hometown, Patchogue, Long Island. Where to begin? There are so many great things about Patchogue. This brief chapter will have to do.

"Matt, each time I think of my hometown, Patchogue High School, Friday night pep rallies, Skyline cheeseburgers, and submarine race-watching as the sun set on the Great South Bay, I feel young, again." Max stifled a chuckle. "Back then, Patchogue had two movie theaters. My favorite was the Rialto."

As we reminisced, Max grew teary-eyed.

"Those years were a special place in time for me too, Max. I'm sorry I didn't know you back then," I said.

One character whom Max had yet to meet was Elmo French, bless his heart. Elmo lived in Patchogue until his parents moved to Brooklyn. Still, every summer Elmo would return to Patchogue and his favorite haunt, Davis Park on Fire Island.

"Tell me about your high school years, Matt."

"Some other time, Max. Let's stick with you story. We have a lot of ground to cover, if we are going to finish your memoir. Let's touch the truly memorable parts," I said.

Max looked askance but continued. "So many wonderful memories. Where to begin?" Max replied.

*   *   *

Max took a deep breath and slowly exhaled. "Alvin's Bar and Grille is as good a place as any to start, Matt."

Here are the highlights of what Max told me.

Alvin's was a waterfront restaurant where Bobby Sugar's cover band gigged on Saturday evenings. With a touch of genius, Bobby named his fifties cover band, Sugar.

There was a time when Alvin's was jumping with locals plus the Friday night Fire Island crowd waiting to catch the Davis Park Ferry. Saturday night was a different story. Nearby Sayville with its many restaurants and boutique shops was the big draw for the fashion conscious revelers departing for Fire Island's fashion center, Cherry Grove.

Max told me that Ed and Alvin, the restaurant owners, were down on their luck. Ed hoped a fifties cover band would attract new customers.

To top the partner's woes, a shocking event took place. Felicia, Ed's wife, a naughty redhead, one might call a gamer, ran off with Alvin. It wasn't the first time Felicia had swapped Ed for another man. In a way, Ed felt relieved to see the last of Felicia except this recent betrayal was with his closest friend and partner, Alvin.

Felicia was a demanding woman with more needs than wants, especially in bed. Regrettably, Alvin's prolonged foreplay belied the evening's promise as he waited for the transformative magic blue pills to kick-in. The tryst turned a bit rough. Three Viagras and a five-hour ecstasy, exacerbated an undetected hole in Alvin's heart. Hence - cardiac distress. An ischemic priapism is not a reward for good behavior or sexual prowess. Peligro! That baby requires immediate medical attention.

Alvin collapsed on top of Felicia. She struggled to call 911. First responders rescued the frantic Felicia. Alvin was lifeless.

A few days later, a repentant Felicia begged to return home, but Ed had endured enough.

As for the restaurant, Bobby Sugar warned Ed, "You are throwing your money way. Ed, the crowd wants a band on Friday night."

Nevertheless, Ed insisted Sugar perform on Saturday evenings. The Saturday night crowd were locals who headed straight for the bar after a Big Mac. The dining room was nearly empty. A cloud of cigarette smoke hung over the bar. That's where Max encountered Elmo French.

* * *

Elmo French looked to be in his late sixties. He dressed like a Hollywood celebrity. This man wore a white linen suit, casual chic pastel peach shirt, and Bugarri elevators. Who couldn't help but notice Elmo?

His appearance demanded fashion savvy. Elmo's persona broadcast, "I'm a person of influence." It also underscored the brilliance of his eccentricity.

When Elmo French entered a room, he captured everyone's attention. In other words, he appeared impeccable with perhaps one distraction. Elmo stood no more than 5'1". The Bugarri elevators added another two inches. In contrast, Elmo's ego stood about six feet tall.

The band was on break. Max was sipping a Captain and Coke.

"Your usual, Mr. French?" asked Cookie, the barmaid. Elmo French was a regular.

Then without warning French gave Max a shove in his

buttocks. French's marble eyes rolled to the top of his head and then side-to-side as he turned to look up at Max.

"Well, are you going to move?" he demanded.

Max didn't budge.

CHAPTER SEVEN

"The Harsh Critique"

Attempting to be nonchalant, the diminutive Elmo French precariously mounted the barstool next to Max. Cookie, the barmaid, poured French his Ketel One martini with three olives straight up.

French's penetrating eyes and knurled nose foretold many fascinating barstool tales. Max found French's smoker's cough and addiction to Marlborough "reds" irritating. The smell of an overflowing ashtray made Max nauseous.

"French? Like in Mary French?" Max asked with a smile. Now, that was a dumb remark. Mary French was a character in Dos Passos' novel. Max was pathetic in social situations.

Once again, French's marbled eyes rolled to the top of his head. He scowled, turned and looked up at Max.

"I don't know Mary French," he replied with a harsh, grating voice. "You're with the band, right?"

"Max Trotter. Pleased to meet you." Max lifted his class, "Cheers."

"Too loud. Your music is too loud." French replied without returning the courtesy of introducing himself. French's slurred words couldn't disguise a slick New York City or Brooklyn braggadocio.

French tilted his head and tossed a quizzical look. "Tell the boys in the band to turn down the volume."French pointed to his ear and shouted , "You'll go deaf!"

Max got the gist.

"You guys should get a gig at West Lake Nursing Home,

across the river." French pointed toward the boat launch. "I suggest you start playing around five. The residents turn in by seven. The crowd's not liquored up, just hooked on sedatives. You can keep the same song list. It will be new for every performance. Then, again, your music might cause panic disorder."

Max shot French a mean look.

"What's the scrunched, angry look for?" French asked. "It's the truth. That crowd won't remember you. No fear of a heckler tossing a beer bottle at your amp."

Max's scowl turned to a look of confusion. *Who the hell is this guy?* And then, without reason, Max laughed.

"I see no humor in your predicament. Do you guys talk to one another? How about occasionally changing key."

Max counter-punched with a sneer.

French ignored Max.

French crushed his cigarette, wheezed, slid off the barstool, and headed for the parking lot.

"Who is that guy?" Max asked Cookie as she freshened his drink.

"That's Elmo French. He is a frustrated musician," she replied with a grin. "He used to be in the business. Elmo worked for one of the top record companies, the digital part dealing with recording artists. I overheard him say he got out just before the digital bubble burst. Not sure what he meant."

French didn't return. Max walked to the window and watched French open the car door, take hold of the steering wheel and hoist himself onto the front seat of what looked like a classic 1953 Buick.

"If he's such a hotshot, why isn't French driving a BMW or Mercedes convertible?" Max asked Cookie. But she was busy rinsing glasses and never heard Max's envy tinged observation. It was probably for the best because by chance the 1953 Buick Super was Max's dream car.

It would be a long time before their paths would cross.

* * *

On his way back to the impromptu stage, Max spotted a couple ensconced at a corner table. The man waved Max over.

"Say, my wife likes your band. She's got a great voice. Could she join you on a number? It's her birthday."

Bobby heard the request. He winked and gave a thumbs-up.

The birthday girl, her name was Jane, wore a blue velvet dress with a plunging neckline. Jane didn't need a great voice. She looked up at Max, and he stared down at her. "Yes," Max stammered.

"My favorite song is 'Be My Baby,'" Jane said.

"You got it," Max responded. He tried to hide his fear of what was to come.

Cover songs are especially tough to play. "Be My Baby" is the Phil Spector, Wall of Sound, all-time classic. The audience had its rhythm and lyrics embedded in their hippocampi.

Bobby sang a few bars of "Happy Birthday." Then he handed Jane the mic.

Suprisingly, she was composed and confident. She cleared her throat. Bobby adjusted his capo. Alex, the drummer and Jim, the bass player, braced themselves. Max played a four-bar into.

It may have been the two Captain and Cokes that Max downed on break, but Jane sounded like the fourth Ronette. Bobby improvised and lead the band back through one more time. It was the craziest thing. Sugar just gave its greatest performance to a nearly empty house.

Jane's husband stood and applauded. He slipped Bobby a ten-buck tip, smiled, and said, "Thanks. I'll take it from here."

Max turned to Bobby and winked. *You bet your ass he'll take it from here. Jane rekindled hubby's flame.*

The enraptured couple departed, and the band packed up.

Thse boys avoided offers to help which could lead to misplaced equipment or damaged instruments. Once the instruments were safely locked in their cars, they headed back inside for a couple of beers.

"Max, please go find Ed. We have three hundred dollars coming," Bobby said.

It was an unusual request since Bobby handled the money. Nonetheless, Max said, "You got it."

Max found Ed in the kitchen. Ed leaned over a counter. His face buried in his cupped hands.

The two men exchanged glances. Ed started to write a check, but hesitated and as promised, he paid in cash.

Bobby bought a round of drinks after the crowd left. They talked about the performance. Max briefly mentioned Elmo French's critique.

The consensus? "Screw that guy."

Ed folded Alvin's that weekend. Sadly, Ed disappeared six months later. Coincidently, Cookie dropped out of sight, too.

"At least we got paid," Bobby reminded Max.

Nevertheless, French's harsh remarks troubled Max. The song list needed revision. Sugar didn't fit in at Alvin's. An empty audience is a downer for any performer.

❈ ❈ ❈

Sugar gave it their best shot the following weekend, at a timeworn hotel known for its Friday night fish fry. The band started playing around 9:30 as the beer and pizza crowd rolled in. The place had a reputation for bar fights. Bobby cautioned the band that the bartender kept a shotgun under the counter. "If he pulls it out, crawl off the stage and get the hell out of here."

"What about the instruments?" Alex, the drummer, asked.

"Screw the instruments. Save your ass," Bobby said.

The louder the disorderly patrons got, the louder the band played. Bobby turned up the volume. Max couldn't hear himself. He didn't care, and nobody else did either. On a rare occasion, Bobby wished the boys were inside a chicken wire cage, but no one threw beer bottles. The rowdy customers loved Sugar.

Surprisingly, Max found fifty bucks and a few Canadian coins in the plastic pretzel container labeled "tip jar." At last, Sugar found a home.

Sugar stopped the mid-week practices. Bobby added a couple of new cover tunes to the song list. All-in-all Bobby didn't give a rat's ass. It was all about having a good time.

One evening the band came to a crossroads.

❊ ❊ ❊

Gus Algrave offered Sugar a gig at his place, "Sweet Toes," a biker bar on the Sunrise Highway. Neither Bobby nor Max had frequented "Sweet Toes." They decided to check it out.

They arrived in separate cars and parked away from the club. They cautiously maneuvered through the maze of motorcycles.

A sign on the door read, "No colors. No weapons."

"Max, I remember this place. Sweet Toes used to be a church," Bobby said.

"Were you an altar boy?" Max asked.

"Max, does it matter?"

"I guess not. But the politically correct term is a

'decommissioned house of worship.' Churches are going out of business all over the country."

"Max, who cares? Now it's a topless bar. The ladies await." Bobby pushed Max through the doorway.

An intense aroma of a marijuana cloud enhanced the biker ambiance. A vast bar stretched the width of the room. On one end was a stage to accommodate a DJ or small band. A brass pole accentuated the décor. Nevertheless, Miss Kitty was Sweet Toes' main attraction.

Miss Kitty picked up a few cast-off miscellanies and sashayed across the bar top. Her destination?

At the far end of the bar stood an opaque shower. Suddenly, an impetuous biker lunged at Miss Kitty and ripped her bra out of her hand.

Gus shouted at the biker to hand over the bra, but the biker shoved the bra in his mouth and tossed Gus the bird. Gus appeared to let the excitement settle down as Miss Kitty stepped into the shower and turned on the water. The attractive young woman and a bar of soap grabbed everyone's attention.

Max and Bobby cautiously worked their way through a maze of howling bikers to get closer to the shower display.

"Holly smokes, Bobby. Is that real soap?" asked Max.

"Who cares? Max. Don't tell me this is your first time at a topless bar."

"Bobby, there is a first time for everything."

But getting back to the big galoot with the bra in his mouth, the drunken fool kicked off his engineer boots, tore off his leather vest, and dropped his pants. His two mates boosted him up on the bar.

The resourceful DJ scrambled to find a rendition of the "Stripper." Someone threw a beer bottle at the dancing fool. The bottle missed him, but smashed the shower door.

Enough was enough. Gus reached under the bar for

his Louisville Slugger. Gus swung at the nearest target, the exhibitionist's right leg. It was a home run. The sound of the baseball bat impacting the dude's leg echoed above the ruckus. The victim's scream was loud, too. He tumbled forward into the crowd. The customers thought the entire show was hilarious.

Gus bulled his way around to the bar unaware of the big lug's two friends. Without warning, as one guy distracted Gus, the other lunged at Gus with a knife. Someone yelled, "He's got a knife." Too late. The son of a bitch missed Gus' back and drove the switchblade into Gus' left buttock.

A chair flew by Max's head. Recalling Bobby's warning about the bartender's shot gun, Max droppped to the floor and crawled behind the bar.

Bobby was right. You can't save your ass and your face at the same time.

Bobby was nowhere in sight. Bobby, the fearless band leader and perfect gentleman, called out to the frantic Miss Kitty to shelter with him. The skirmish continued for another 30 minutes. Bobby, Max and and the luscious Miss Kitty were huddled in Bobby's car. Naturally, Bobby offered the water soaked and shivering Miss Kitty an old Army blanket to stay warm.

The cops and ambulances finally arrived. Gus and the injured biker were transported to Brookhaven Hospital. Bobby crept back inside, grabbed Miss Kitty's purse and dressing robe and vamoosed.

A few days later, Bobby called. Along with Miss Kitty, the boys in the band decided to move to Milwaukee. Why?

At first, I couldn't figure it out. There was no way I was leaving Patchogue. The real story?

Miss Kitty's boyfriend, a psychopath, was hunting for Bobby Sugar and the buxom twenty-year-old, Miss Kitty.

✳ ✳ ✳

"It's been a while since I visited Patchogue, Matt. I miss Alvin's and the Davis Park Ferry crowd. Alvin's was demolished to expand the ferry parking lot."

"Follow your dreams,
reach for the stars...
but never forget
where you come from."
Anonymous

CHAPTER EIGHT

"Let The Adventure Begin. Meet Max Trotter's Entourage."

Yesterday, Max told me about his first meeting with Elmo French's companions, Dawn and Deidre Skipper, the precocious twenty-four-year-old twins. Here's what Max told me.

"Matt, I stopped at Jugz the other evening for a quick Sassy after a long day researching at the library. The drive-thru line wrapped around the building. I hurried inside to place my order. As luck would have it, Elmo French was holding court at a table in the far corner, surrounded by his coterie of two attractive coeds.

I tried to avoid eye contact. Elmo was dazzling the two impressionable young women with tales of past glories.

Too late. Elmo saw me and invited me to his table. "Sorry, Elmo. I can't stay."

"Nonsense, Max. We were discussing memoir when your name came up. I was bragging about you. I told them about your memoir."

Elmo pointed to his table. "The young lady with dark glasses wants to study memoir. She could benefit from your experience," Elmo said.

At that point, vanity got the best of me. I grabbed my coffee and followed Elmo.

He introduced me to Deidre and Dawn Skipper. I suspected Elmo prided himself with challenging propriety. He breached a perilous boundary with the Skipper twins. His female neighbors were scandalized by Elmo's behavior while he was envied by men of all ages. And Elmo liked it that way.

Elmo had become reckless since his wife, Sylvia, ran off with her yogi. But that's another story.

"My friend, Max, is an accomplished musician and writer," Elmo said.

Dawn, the the youngest identical twin, forced a smile and leaned across the table toward Elmo. For a moment I felt myself gawking. Dawn was incredible in that braless tank top. The way she twirled a straw in her ice mocha beguiled me.

Deidre, the older twin, removed her dark glasses revealing captivating blue eyes that could derail a freight train. "What made you return to school to study memoir at your age?" Deidre asked.

That was a mouthful, especially the "at your age" part. "I didn't return to school to study memoir. I wanted to study anthropomorphic taxidermy. The class was closed. And so, I enrolled in Memoir Writing."

Elmo snickered. Dawn looked perplexed.

Deidre asked, "Anthropomorphic taxidermy? I never heard of it. Is it like an esthetician?"

"Hmm…well, not quite," I replied. I could see Elmo was paying attention to me, and Dawn was annoyed.

Elmo winked and said, "Tell us more, Max."

"OK. When I was young, my parents wanted me to be a mortician and maybe own a funeral home like my Uncle John. We lived on the second floor of Uncle John's funeral home. At an early age, I disliked dead people. Besides, from any perspective, embalming can be a messy profession."

Deidre and Dawn seemed drawn into my story.

"What was it like?" asked Dawn.

"It was hushed. We always spoke in whispers, even when the place was empty. Uncle John wouldn't allow my school friends to visit, so I wrote short stories, created imaginary friends, and practiced piano. Most of all, I liked making dioramas. We didn't have TV, Facebook, or video games."

"Dioramas, like museum displays?" asked Dawn. Her response kind of impressed me.

"Yes, but on a much smaller scale," I said. Elmo was struggling to stifle his laughter.

"So, what did your dioramas display?" Dawn asked. But this time her question sounded like a smart-assed third grader wanting to know how much the earth would weigh without people.

"My Uncle John was a cleanliness nut. You must be, especially in the mortuary. You can't have mice and bugs climbing over the cadavers."

"Max, I'll pay twenty-five cents for every mouse you catch, but dead, not alive," Uncle John offered.

"Twenty-five cents was a lot of money when I was a kid. After a while, I was earning two dollars a week. There was one problem."

"What?" asked Deidre.

"What to do with the dead mice? Watching Uncle John embalming old Mr. Hassle, it came to me. On rainy days, Uncle John taught me basic taxidermy. It opened a whole new hobby and brought my imaginary friends to life. Well, not quite."

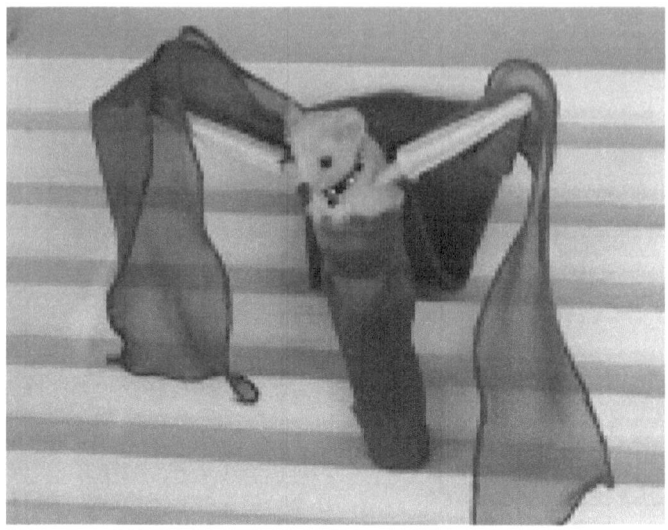

Dawn scowled.

"The taxidermist, not only works towards a lifelike appearance, but his work is intended for display."

Deidre's jaw dropped, and her mouth opened wide in disbelief.

"Excuse me, folks," said Elmo, hysterically laughing. But I continue.

"Each time I had a couple of mice sewed up and preserved, mother would make the cutest costumes. I built several dioramas from cardboard. My favorite was the Alexander Hamilton-Aaron Burr duel."

"The one where Burr kills Hamilton?" asked smarty-pants Dawn.

"That's the one," I said with a wink. The couple at the neighboring table eavesdropped. But I continued.

"Then, Mom surprised me on my first Thanksgiving home from college."

"How so?" smug Dawn asked.

"Mom gathered all my mice and dressed them as Pilgrims and Indians. It was the centerpiece of the Thanksgiving table. What a treat."

"Mister, that's disgusting," shouted the woman at the other table. The couple dragged their screaming child out the door.

"How could you be so horrid," scolded Dawn shoving Deidre to move along. "Tell Elmo we'll see him later."

*　*　*

"Mother created the cutest costumes."
Max Trotter

The Christmas Spirit
Photograph of Sak's Fifth Ave.

CHAPTER NINE

"Spot and Puff."

The setting: Jugz around 8:00 PM. The narrator, Matt Nagle.

After reading Max's tale of mice collecting, I thought you might like another anecdote. This one may give you an insight into Max Trotter's backstory.

Young Max and his parents lived in Uncle John's Serenity Funeral Home.

"Uncle John was very strict," Max told me.

"When I was a kid, I wanted a pet. If only we lived in a traditional home, just like ordinary folks, I could have enjoyed the companionship of a cuddly puppy or kitten. "But we lived with Uncle John in a two-story funeral home.

"No pets!" Uncle John shouted. "And that's the end of it."

Uncle John took exception to dogs barking and cat hair in the viewing area he called the parlor. My father was a kind-hearted man. Sadly, living in the funeral home had altered his personality. While assisting the deceased's family make necessary arrangement, and selecting a coffin, my father was always helpful and never steered them toward lavish expenses. Regrttably, he was always timid and obedient when dealing with his brother, my Uncle John. And my mother, too, for that matter.

One day, dad said to my mother, "Damn it Erica, if Max

wants a pet, he's going to have one."

"Calm down, Burt. Don't do something rash," my mother urged.

That night, my dad, after a few Jamesons, worked up enough courage to defy Uncle John, Several days later, two large boxes arrived.

"I was puzzled. What a surprise. Dad and I opened the boxes. Holy smokes! I'll always remember the proud smile on my father's face as I opened the gift boxes. Dad had beaten Uncle John at his game and gifted me years of fun. Finally, pets of my own - Spot and Puff - taxidermied in their final glory."

Spot was a mutt that dad swore was a terrier in his other life. I was convinced that Spot was the victim of a hit-and-run. Spot's hips looked odd, mounted on a plywood platform with wobbly wheels.

"I could never pull Spot too far before he fell over. I dragged him until there was little left of the old boy. I loved Spot," Max recalled.

"Don't drag that damn thing on the hardwood floors," Uncle John scolded.

"By the time I was ten, Spot had seen better days. Dad and I buried Spot in the backyard one evening while Uncle John was busy in the mortuary. I still have Puff, an orange-colored tabby. I'm not much of a cat lover. I keep her in a storage box under my bed."

* * *

"The road to hell is paved with unsold stuffed dogs."
Ernest Hemingway

CHAPTER TEN

"A Rainy Day Reunion."

Greetings. It's me again, Matt Nagle, your narrator and editor. My former wife, Elizabeth, decided we'd move to Deepmarsh Village, a small community a few miles from Fairden, South Carolina. Fairden is a unique and picturesque city, quiet and safe, not unlike Aiken or Bluffton. Like any small residential community, Fairden had its ups and downs. It all began when Sherman marched through here.

Most recently we made national news when the Fairden City Council purchased an abandoned paper mill for one dollar but spent millions turning it into a park. What a deal.

Who knew it had been a chemical waste dump? Fairden's Memorial Park was number eleven on the top twenty Superfund Sites, just below the decaying Savannah River Nuclear Plant.

Luckily, the disaster turned into a tourist gold mine like Chernobyl. Fairden no longer depended on speed traps. In other words, today Fairden is a safe and financially sound community. I called Fairden South Carolina's "sweet spot."

Except for the Freeport Hotel Grille, a few restaurants, and Jugz, the town closes down around nine PM, Fairden's midnight. You'll find the closest nightlife in Millcreek Commons, about 10 miles from here. They have a Giant14 Theater and a Barnes & Noble Bookstore. Now Fairden also has Emma's Bookstore.

* * *

One rainy morning, I found myself at Barnes & Noble sipping a mocha latte and browsing books.

Since Sandra and I opened Emma's Bookstore in Fairden, I frequent Barnes & Noble a couple of times a month to check their inventory and endcaps. I'm an elite browser. I can read a novel over a couple of cups of java and never buy the book. I'd bet, Barnes & Noble rakes in more money from coffee than hardcover book sales.

I recently finished Orwell's *1984*, and sex was on my mind. I browsed the self-improvement stacks.

"Can I help you find a book?" asked one of the employees.

"Oh no. Just browsing. Thanks," I said.

The young man looked at me and then pointed to the stacks. And in all youthful innocence, he declared, "We just opened a new section you might find interesting."

He undoubtedly caught me tilting my head, a habit I've acquired when I am curious. Needless to say, he continue his pitch.

"Books on sex and health for folks over sixty are among our best sellers. I unpacked ten new ones yesterday."

"Thanks for the information," I whispered and motioned for the young man to lower his voice. Discussing sexual intimacy and aging were taboos I shared with my former wife.

"I can tell you are a true book lover," the young man said.

"How so?"

"I watched you sniffing and thumbing your way through a book. I think is was, *You And Your Colonoscopy*. Was it interesting?"

I tossed the young man a puzzled look. "I appreciate your help," I replied politely, shooing the kid in the opposite direction.

I looked around. The aisle between the stacks was empty, so I removed my hat and sunglasses. I ran my fingers over the book spines as though instinctively I could connect telepathically with the author. A yellow and red cover attracted my attention. The title shouted, *Incendiary Sex and the Best Positions.*

I hesitated. *Sounds great, but what are sex tantras?* I was about to replace the book when I heard a familiar voice.

"Matt Nagle. Nothing like Barnes & Nobel on a rainy day." It was Max Trotter.

"There's always Emma's Bookstore. And we appreciate your patronage," I replied using my library voice.

Max looked at the section sign – "Sex Over Sixty."

"Stop right there, Max. Don't say a word."

"Nonsense. I was about to say that bright people think alike," Max said as he took the book out of my hand, glanced at the title, and said, "Tantric sex doesn't work for me, Matt. I'm not into slow, meditative sex. Supposedly the goal is not orgasm but enjoying transformational sexual energy. But that's all bullshit. I want to feel like I'm popping the cork on a bottle of champagne. Sure, I wish the ride would last longer than 30 seconds, but at my age, I'll take what I can get."

"Hey, I never pictured you as the kind of a guy who likes sexual yoga positions."

"Max, that sounds like gross locker room talk to me," I replied.

"I've been loading up with male supplements and waiting for the right moment," said Max flexing his left arm.

"Too much anticipation for a sixty-second pop," I said with a chuckle.

"Matt, here's one that should appeal to you, *Soft Sex,*" Max replied as he shoved the book at me.

"Touché, Max."

Then I whispered, "I am getting a bit horny. My divorce was finalized about a year ago. I'm not dating. Don't want any commitments."

"I'm sorry for taunting you, old man. As a divorce expert, I damn well know the inevitabilities of bachelor asceticism," Max said. "When you finish browsing meet me at the coffee bar. Max pointed to the far side of the store. By the way, Matt. I asked the clerk about your last novel."

"And?"

"The last copy of *Brandi Barton* is on the 50% discount table."

I scowled and walked toward the table. The book was gone.

About thirty minutes later, I found Max sitting at an empty table. I ordered two chai teas, or is it two tai chis?

CHAPTER ELEVEN

"Speak Of The Devil."

A tap on the shoulder interrupted our conversation. Max glanced around, and to his surprise, it was Elmo French. French was the character Max encountered at Alvin's Restaurant, years ago, back in Patchogue.

French dressed dapper as ever but absent the white linen suit. From Max's description, I'd recognize Elmo French anywhere.

Today's ensemble, white linen. There was something about French and white linen, and pastel blue shirttails hanging out. I noted the sockless Tom's light tan canvas stitch-outs. Of course, he wore the trademark white Kogol in reverse.

"May I join you?" Elmo asked.

"Of course."

A surprised Max motioned for Elmo to sit down.

"Mr. French, I'm surprised you remembered me." Max recalled their last conversation.

"Please call me Elmo, though I would like my future wife to call me Mr. French rather than a few of her nicknames for me. Max, your band was unforgettable and unforgivable," the stone-faced Elmo responded.

Max anticipated Elmo's caustic remark.

I felt a bit awkward. "Excuse me," I said.

"Oh, Matt, forgive me. "Elmo, meet Matt Nagle. Matt's a starving author."

I shot back a quizzical look. *Where's Max headed with that remark?*

"Self-published?" Elmo looked at me for a second.
I nodded.

"Marketing, Nagle. In today's world, you can sell shit; it just takes a spin. All you need is the right sales pitch—the bigger the lie, the better. The world loves bullshit. People don't go beyond the headlines, if they get that far. The lies spread quickly while the truth limps after it. As for me, I only lie when I have to."

I heard that before but I can't recall who said it. Still, I started to respond when Elmo interrupted.

"Everyone is publishing a book, Nagle. The average reading level has decreased from eighth grade to seventh. Folks blame it on the Covid lockdown." (*Editor's note: To avoid pedantry, I've gone with "Covid" as opposed to "COVID" or COVID-19 when referring to the coronavirus.)*

I was stunned by Elmo's gruffness. Max, on the other hand, laughed his ass off. *What's so funny?*

Elmo turned to Max. "Like my Tom's? Buy one, and they ship another pair to poor kids. My parents were always promoting the poor starving kids in China. We have poor kids in LA, Patchogue, and Sheboygan."

Immediately I suspected that Elmo was an effete snob. I let his comment slide.

"So, how's the band doing, Joe?" Elmo asked.

"It's not Joe, Mr. French. My name is Max Trotter."

"Sure, sure. I apologize. I struggle with your face, but who could forget your voice? So, how's the band doing, Max?" Elmo tauntingly asked.

Max looked at me for support.

Elmo is busting Max's balls, so I held back to enjoy the banter. But what's this business about a band? I didn't know Max Trotter had a band. And why does Max insist on calling this guy Mr. French rather than Elmo?

"The band broke up," Max said.

"That's a pleasant thought," Elmo replied. "I tried to warn you, but you were too defensive. I've been around LA,

New York City, Nashville, Atlanta, and even London for a long time. Promotion. The whole side of what is quickly becoming a crumbling industry. I've produced several top bands. Believe me. You guys were beating up on some great cover tunes."

"Is that why you left Alvin's that night and stuck me with the bar bill?"

"You deserved to pay. You got your money's worth, Joe." Elmo persisted on badgering Max.

"It's Max. And I'll admit I thought about what you said. But it's your attitude," Max insisted. "It's like you're rebounding from an argument with your wife and taking it out on me. I know the feeling."

"I'm not married—my wife's deceased."

"Sorry. But you seem to be an unhappy man, and the last thing I need is bad karma," Max added.

I was confused. Bad karma? Where the hell is Max going with this?

I watched Elmo push his chair away from the table. "I'm bad karma? Back in Manhattan or LA, a guy like you would be camped outside my office begging me to promote his band. I wasn't giving you advice. I was providing constructive criticism. You should be paying me."

I patiently watched and waited as Max and Elmo bantered.

"Excuse me, gentlemen, but I'm getting a refill. Elmo would you care for a latté?" *I needed to get away from those two.*

"I'll take you up on your offer with one reservation. Next time I'll pay."

That was a unique way of encouraging me to pick up the tab.

I smiled and nodded in agreement.

Elmo glanced across the room and then checked his mobile phone. "I'm here with a friend. She drove. She's browsing. She reads self-help books and personal lifestyle stuff, like yoga and running. Right now, she's in a spiritual mode. But that's fine by me," Elmo said with a shrug.

I returned with the refills and the conversation continued.

As we talked, I sensed we might be meeting Elmo again.

"Elmo, have you lived in South Carolina for a long time?" I inquired.

"Off and on. I play a little golf. I'm renting in Deepmarsh Village."

Max looked surprised. "I live there, too."

French raised one eyebrow and replied, "We're renting. I want to build the biggest and most expensive home in the neighborhood. I deserve it. Sadly, I'm constantly running afoul of the Architectural Review Board. I'm tossing in the towel and moving to an exclusive gated community a few miles from Deepmarsh."

"What about you, Matt?"

"I live in a condo near the river. Small, but it's all a bachelor needs."

French paused to reflect. He peered into his latté. "I'm mostly retired. Left the music industry several years back—time flies. You know how that goes. Invested my retirement incentive into a couple of enterprises."

I felt a bit uncomfortable. No, I don't know how that goes, Elmo. I can't imagine what it's like to be a millionaire.

"So, how did you wind up here in Fairden?" I inquired without appearing to nosy.

"Like I told you. I invested in several businesses with a friend and purchased a restaurant. A gorgeous creature, my friend, that is. And she's bright, too," Elmo quickly added, looking around as though someone might be listening. "I'm a bit gun gun shy when it comes to inclusive language. I find that constantly refering to my politically correct inclusive language guide restricts conversation."

French paused to gather his thought and said, "But getting back to the restaurant, I rarely go there. Alice would put me to work. Standing on my feet for 14 hours a day would exhaust me. It's Alice's restaurant. I also own the Salon

Beauté a few doors away from Emma's Bookstore. The salon should be opened for business any time now."

"Of course, now I recall your name. I'm part-owner of Emma's," I said.

"As for the coffee shop, that project should be underway. I've secured the boardwalk location and permits. My dream is to own a primo café. Elegant, but with a local flavor."

"Sounds like you're enjoying semi-retirement," said Max.

"For a while, I went into a funk. I didn't exactly retire. I took the incentive and ran. Never went back," Elmo recalled.

I was surprised by Elmo's candor.

"What happened?"

❋ ❋ ❋

"How queer everything is today!

And yesterday things went on just as usual. I wonder if I've been changed in the night. Let me think: was I the same when I got up this morning?

I almost think I can remember feeling a little different. But if I'm not the same the next question is, *'Who in the world am I?'* Ah, that's the great puzzle!"

Lewis Carroll

CHAPTER TWELVE

"The Suits"

Elmo pushed his cup aside and leaned into the table. He looked intense. "In brief, the recording industry I grew up in was changing," Elmo explained. "Things were happening too fast. Put it this way: I felt like I was standing on a subway platform waiting for my connection. The trains kept passing through the station without stopping. Each train moved a little faster. It was a recurring dream, an unsettling nightmare."

Elmo recalled being caught up in the technological advances. "Tape cassettes were vanishing along with the Walkman. The compact disc was headed for extinction. I have a suspicious mind. I can't prove it, but I suspect the auto makers conspired to remove CD players from cars to cut costs."

"Maybe the big music labels had something up their sleeves," Max added.

"The technology revolution disrupted the industry and angered consumers. Their CDs were obsolete. Streaming," Elmo said. "First it was CD's then DVD's."

Elmo was growing intense. "Who knows what would have happened if it weren't for Michael Jackson and Mariah Carey? They gave the business a temporary breather."

"It happened anyway. I have tons of CDs," I added.

Elmo appeared to enter a contemplative state as he recounted the events. "My father, God bless him, cautioned me to leave at the top of my game. That was good advice."

"My dad said something like that too," I agreed.

"I had a comfortable office in one of the two Madison Avenue buildings and a suite in LA," Elmo claimed with a touch of braggadocio.

Then Elmo related his daunting story. "It was Christmas time. The company threw a Christmas party for the digital guys at a plush Manhattan restaurant. It was one of those parties where up until a few years ago, it was okay to mess around with your secretary and blame it on the alcohol and a couple of snorts. I was obligated to attend."

Max looked at me as though he anticipated an insider's scandalous revelation.

Elmo continued. "Standing at the far end of the bar, I watched two 'suits,' the hot shots from our accounting department. We called these young guys 'suits' because they dressed well and laughed at the boss' jokes, but they didn't know shit about marketing. And our bottom line showed it."

"Max and I agree on how important marketing is," I said.

Elmo went on. "One of the suits claimed to have scored with an intern. He was loud. Anyway, the other guy said something like 'probably Monday.'" I didn't know what they were talking about. I didn't know shit." Elmo pounded his fist on the table so hard his latte splashed.

"The following Monday morning, I was summoned to a briefing. Corporate is downsizing. 'We need this handled expeditiously.' I was ordered to finish the first round by December 31," an angry Elmo growled. "The company closed our division and outsourced the work to India. I didn't see it coming. I was too close."

"Firing people at Christmas?" I asked.

"That's how the bottom-line works. They decided, 'We needed to clean up our act before New Year's Eve.'"

"Clean up our act? You mean to dump a couple of hundred people? Cost cutting looks good in the annual report," Elmo replied.

"A couple of hundred?" Max asked.

"Hell, that was only the tip of the iceberg. What about all

the contractors and the independent vendors?" I asked.

"So, ultimately what was your role in all this?""Max asked.

"Thinking back, I'm not too sure. I just had to be there when the shit hit the fan. There were tears, rage, indifference, threats, and every imaginable emotion."

"Did you ever hear from any of your staff?" I asked.

"A few, but my immediate staff was pissed thinking I knew about the layoffs. The top executives had nondisclosure agreements and huge bonuses. Others were lucky to get severance pay and medical. The remaining employees received job counseling. Oh, I received a few calls from headhunters about one or two of my staff. My company avoided letters of reference. And once the circus left town, it was my turn. I could have remained a year or two longer, but I knew my time was coming. So I bailed with a surprisingly generous parachute."

"It must have been a nightmare," Max said.

Elmo turned in his seat and tossed his cup into the garbage can. "That's about it," he said.

Elmo's an odd duck. Complicated. Aren't we all? Sometimes supportive and at times angry. Moody too.

Reluctantly, I found Elmo French was growing on me.

❈ ❈ ❈

"What goes around comes around." In 2022, Taylor Swift's Midnights became the first major album release to have its vinyl sales outpace CD's since 1987.

Kenna McCafferty, "Taylor Swift is Bringing Vinyl Back."

CHAPTER THIRTEEN

"Meet Sylvia"

Out of the corner of my eye I saw a gorgeous woman approaching our table. "There your are, Elmo. You promised to meet me at the rear entrance. Well?" She smiled and said, "Since Elmo is gauche, I'll introduce myself. Hi. I'm Sylvia."

"I apologize, my dear. Meet Max Trotter and Matt Nagle."

Sylvia leaned over to place her packages on an empty chair.

Her shoulder-length blonde hair and the hint of braless nipples pressing through a sheer cotton dress gave Sylvia the appearance of a flower child. Sylvia was a dead ringer for the actress Robin Wright, the captivating Jenny in *Forrest Gump.*

Sylvia looked at least twenty years French's junior. An eye-catcher, she stood nearly six feet tall in her flats, making Elmo French appear even shorter than his 5'1".

I smiled and attempted to stand. "Pleased to meet you," I said.

I stifled a giggle while watching Max absorb Sylvia's assets. *He's going to wrench his neck if he strains any harder.* Max appeared mesmerized by Sylvia's cleavage.

Sylvia caught Max's admiring peek.

"Not *the* Max Trotter from Long Island?" Sylvia asked.

"Why, yes, that's me," Max stammered. Sylvia caught him off guard.

"Elmo tends to be a curmudgeon. It was your band. You nearly drove him insane that night. I pride myself in all aspects of calming techniques. As hard as I tried, nothing soothed Elmo that night."

Max shrugged and turned red with embarrassment.

"Now, Elmo. Gather these packages, and we are off. Another week and I'll be Mrs. French, again."

I caught the grimace that flashed across Elmo's face.

"Divorces take so long in South Carolina. My other two came off like clockwork. This one's a hassle. Right, Elmo? Elmo probably told you I was the first Mrs. French. I was just seventeen. You know what I mean? Like robbing the cradle. Right dear? Elmo likes them young. A regular John Derek."

Elmo flushed.

"I didn't mean to embarrass you."

"You did. I hardly know these men, and you're revealing intimacies."

"Darling, you know your temper arouses me." Sylvia bent over to give Elmo a consoling peck on his cheek.

Klaatu barada nikto! I felt my eyes were going to pop out of my head.

Max white-knuckled the table.

"Sylvia, please," Elmo protested as she nuzzled closer.

I imagined the pair under the influence of a few dry martinis. Sylvia was in the driver's seat. And why not?

"We've got to run, darling." Sylvia playfully tugged at his ear.

"Trotter, I'm getting married or rather re-married next week. Here's my card. If you decide to assemble a garage band, give me a call. Here's one for you too, Matt."

"Thanks, Elmo, but my garage band days are over."

Sylvia smiled and said, "Music, marketing, and sex. Elmo is possessed. I'm exhausted. On the other hand, being married to a multi-millionaire has its rewards."

Sylvia flashed an engagement ring that must have cost five hundred grand, and laughing offered, "Take him to lunch or whatever. Get him out of the house. He's driving me crazy."

✻ ✻ ✻

"Train yourself to let go of everything you fear to lose."

Anonymous

CHAPTER FOURTEEN

"Matt and Max Visit Elmo French."

Max Trotter and Elmo French acted like they were highrollers. Looking around my sparsely furnished condo, I questioned my hasty decision to relinquish my home in Deepmarsh Village. Living alone is quite an adjustment. My income was cut in half.

One afternoon, I found Elmo French's business card in my bulky wallet. Perhaps from loneliness, I gave French a call. Sylvia answered.

"Stop by, Matt," Sylvia said. "Elmo enlarged the master bedroom deck. Contractors are working, so there is a lot of commotion."

That didn't matter. I called Max. "Sure let's go," he agreed." I drove. We were both anxious to see Elmo's home and Sylvia too.

Elmo and Sylvia now lived in Sweet Water, where the least expensive home cost nearly two million dollars. A visitor's pass was waiting for us at the gate. Driving over the bridge, I felt the ambiance of living rich. Max found the address.

"By god! There it is. I'd know that car anywhere," Max exclaimed.

"Max, that's a Mercedes Benz S-Class. Can you imagine how much it cost?"

"Not the Mercedes, Matt. The other sedan. It's a 1953 Buick Super Sedan. Look at those spoke wheels. You can't get better than that."

"But the front grill, Max. It's so ugly," I replied.

"You don't know cars, Matt. That 1953 Buick Super is a

classic. Elmo owned that gem when I first met him years ago in Patchogue."

"Never saw one before."

"That's because most of them were junked. Today, they sell for thousands of dollars, if you can find one. Ooops. There's Sylvia." I point to the front porch.

Sylvia greeted us.

"It's a beautiful home, Sylvia." Max wasn't kidding. The home was a true-to-life cover shot from *Southern Living.*

Sylvia stepped forward and gave each of us a peck on the check. She wore a skimpy nighty that caught my eye.

"Forgive my appearance, gentlemen, but I forgot that Elmo and I have a luncheon date this afternoon. I'm about ready to step into the shower."

Sylvia's apology was unnecessary. Her nightie and intoxicating fragrance granted her absolution. My adolescent mind was running amuck. *The first look was for me. The second look was for the Devil.*

Sylvia, nearly six feet tall, and Elmo made a physically contrasting couple. I scolded myself for wondering what those two were like in bed. I guessed Sylvia had caught my gaze.

"I know what you're thinking, Matt."

"You do?" *I hoped I wasn't that obvious.*

"Why do two people need a five-bedroom home? This whole place was Elmo's idea, right down to the splash pad shower with the built-in love seat. Undeniably, it's more comfortable than doing it on an ordinary shower floor. I'm through with that. We all know that men are not created equally," Sylvia continued. "Some are bigger than others. Besides, Elmo's behavior in the shower doesn't quite conform to what you would expect from a man twice his size. Elmo truly loves me. Tell me gentlemen, do you find my beauty and size, intimidating?" Sylvia asked.

Max looked at me and smiled.

Where is she going with this?

Sylvia tied the tiny blue ribbon at the top of her nightie as a gesture of modesty.

* * *

Sylvia insisted on giving us the grand tour. The bedroom was in disarray. Sylvia picked up one or two intimate items and quickly tossed them in a drawer.

"Wow. Those ceiling mirrors must have cost a fortune," said Max with a Cheshire cat grin.

I walked into the sunroom and looked to my right. Two huge, cast iron four-legged bathtubs sat outside the master bedroom's sliding glass doors. The plumber smiled at Silvia as he finished installing the faucets.

"Holy smokes. Look at those bath tubs!" I was amazed. *Straight out of the Cialis ad, but twice as big.*

"Oh, Matt, please don't call them bath tubs when Elmo's around. Elmo dubbed them the 'Love Tubs.' He's so silly. It's ridiculous. One night we're watching TV, and the Cialis commercial came on. You know, the one where a couple in separate tubs watch the sunset. And as I recall, the woman asks, 'Darling, did you remember to take your pill?'"

"That's the ad," Max said.

"I can't figure out why we needed two tubs. Elmo always climbs in with me." Sylvia chuckled.

"I'm completely baffled," replied Max.

"And so is Elmo. He started babbling about lovers in separate tubs. Elmo is so impulsive. The next thing I know, these tubs were delivered—what a job. The porch needed a steel girder added to support the damn things. The company used a crane to hoist the tubs over the roof and guide them to the deck. The neighbors were pissed. Oh well, anything to keep my man happy. Right, Max?" Sylvia caught the daydreaming Max off guard.

I gave Max a nudge. *I'll bet he was dreaming about soaking with Sylvia.*

Sylvia moved closer to me. I felt my face turning red.

"Matt, I learned the hard way. No man stays with a woman for bad sex. Elmo treats me well. And vice versa."

Sylvia held up her left hand and flashed a striking blueish Tanzanite gem half the size of my fist. "I reciprocate," Sylvia seductively whispered.

A voice boomed from the intercom. "Trotter, Nagle, I've been waiting for you. Stop gawking at my gorgeous wife and get up here."

"Elmo, you old fool. These gentlemen appreciate my intellectual beauty," Sylvia called out as she led us to a staircase at the far end of the house.

"Elmo's in his cave. I don't go up there. It's a mess." Sylvia pointed. "Upstairs and to the left."

Elmo met us at the top of the staircase.

"Trotter, Nagle, good to see you. What do you think of the house?"

"Great," I replied. Elmo's gracious greeting surprised me. We hadn't spoken for months.

This sure is a swell home, Elmo," Max said.

"It's a bit large for us. Our first home was a tiny ranch. I thought we enjoyed a good life. Then, Sylvia left me to find herself on a spiritual voyage to India. The guru was screwing her."

Elmo's candor made me feel uncomfortable.

"It all started at an ashram in the Berkshires. She lived there for a while; meditation and yoga. Every few weeks, I'd send her a check. One night she called asking permission to sleep with the guru." Elmo scrunched his lips.

"So, Max, what brings you here today? Ah, don't tell me. Let me guess."

Max started to answer, but Elmo cut him off.

"You want to start a band. Right?"

Max looked flabbergasted.

Elmo began to lecture. "The first thing you must do is focus on your music, and practice. That's why you need me, Max. You focus on the music. I'll take care of the small stuff."

"I'm not here to start a band or go on the road. I enjoyed talking with you that morning at Barnes & Noble."

"Today's visit was my idea, Elmo," I replied. "I wanted to see your beautiful home. I asked Max to come along."

"Really?"

Then Max chimed in. "Granted, I have been tinkering with forming a garage band for over-the-hill-guys; older guys like me. No more drama and ego conflicts. A fun band for jamming."

"That's not possible. It's bound to get serious, like a cough morphing into pneumonia. It's a matter of discipline," replied the crafty Elmo.

"I don't want to be serious. I want to have fun."

"So, are you asking me to help start a garage band? That's a first for me."

"A simple garage band. I'm not looking to be the opener for the Rolling Stones," said Max.

"I get your point," Elmo replied.

"Perhaps when the time comes you can assist me to put something together. Do you want to help me?"

"It doesn't matter if you're a garage band or on the road. It would be best if you played well. Know your craft. Then things start to fall into place. You build credibility and respect. And smile a bit. Max, you frown a lot," said Elmo.

"I'm not looking to impress. I just want to have fun. If it isn't fun, I don't want to do it," Max insisted.

Without skipping a beat, Elmo looked at me. The discussion took a detour. "Matt, where's your wedding band? You were wearing it when we had coffee."

The question caught me off guard.

"Hold on, Elmo. Where are you going with this?" I

asked.

"Oh, come on. Max told me you are divorced."

I turned and shot an evil eye at Max. I felt defensive.

"Matt, I'll wager you are Catholic. You Catholics are so serious. You can't let go of your ex-wife. Believe me. She has let go of you."

I squirmed. *Elmo has some balls bringing my personal life into the conversation.* I grew angry.

"Divorce hurts. There's no place to run, no place to hide. Music, Matt. Hey, why not help Max form a garage band? But get your head together first."

I looked directedly into Elmo's eyes and told him, "Let's reach an understanding Elmo. Keep, religion, politics and complaints about erectile dysfunction out of our conversations. And that goes for my personal life, too. Stick with the garage band and not marriage counseling." *I felt better getting over that hurdle.*

Elmo frowned, but quickly regained his composure. "Fair enough. I've been there and done that." Elmo shrugged and looked at me with a degree of indifference.

Suddenly from the foot of the staircase came a howl. "Elmo. Get your ass down here. We'll be late," Sylvia roared.

Max was startled.

I was feeling uncomfortable and began fidgeting.

Elmo signaled me to calm down. "Sylvia can be cantankerous. Let's wait for her to start up the stairs." He giggled.

I felt anxious.

"Elmo!" Sylvia called, again.

Elmo help his index finger against his lips and whispered, "I refuse to answer Sylvia unless she uses the intercom."

"Elmo, how did you and Sylvia get back together?" asked Max.

"Facebook, Max. I found her on Facebook one day. And something happened."

"What?"

"I fell in love with her all over again. Who can resist the sparkle in Sylvia's blue eyes?"

"You're a lucky man," I said.

"She's in fantastic shape," Max exclaimed. "Very healthy."

I smiled in agreement, but with a degree of embarassment, too. Max has few filters, and I never know what he might say, especially in social situations. He means well, bless his heart.

"Sylvia claims she remarried me because of my karma. Karma be damned. Sylvia is a pragmatic Buddhist. She likes diamonds and Tanzanite."

I found it puzzling that Elmo fell for his ex-wife on Facebook.

"Elmo let's get going," Sylvia shouted from downstairs.

"Elmo, Sylvia sounds quite anxious," Max said.

"She'll calm down, Max. Give her a moment. It's her ritual."

Then over the intercom came the voice of a gentler and kinder Sylvia. "Elmo, darling. It's time to go. We'll be late."

Elmo chuckled. "Sylvia is a master manipulator, Max. Truthfully, I like it. Still, a man needs to set boundaries for sexual manipulation. I know my weaknesses. So, I allow Sylvia to lead me around on a short leash. It's my way of being in charge," Elmo bragged.

Elmo had a deep intuitive understanding of women quite different from mine.

We thanked Elmo and said goodbye to Sylvia. Two huge pear-shaped diamonds dangled a silly millimeter above her cleavage. The pair mesmerized me.

❊ ❊ ❊

"Elmo treats me well. I reciprocate." Sylvia waved her hand to flash a striking blueish Tanzanite gem half the size of my fist."

Sylvia French

CHAPTER FIFTEEN

"The Unfortunate Text Message."

This scene takes place at Jugzjava.

Max and I found Elmo sulking at a corner table. "So, what's troubling you, Elmo?" Max asked.

"Nothing," Elmo replied, slurping his coffee. "Except, this coffee is too damn hot."

"Don't avoid the question, Elmo. Something is wrong. Your scowl. It's begging me to ask you. So, what's up?" I asked.

"Oh, I'm feeling a bit melancholy. Why did I marry Sylvia for a second time? All she cares about is jewelry and sex. I can't satisfy her. She tossed me on the kitchen floor and demanded an orgasm the other night. What an animal. She's insatiable. I suspect she's getting ready to leave me again. A stretch of rough sex always preceded her departures. I can't deal with the anxiety."

"Elmo, you forgave Sylvia. You remarried her. It's nearly two years since your second wedding. What were you thinking?" I asked.

"Don't remind me. I never learn, Matt."

"There must have been a lot of issues behind your first split."

"You're right, Max. One that stands out."

"What was it?"

Elmo paused and whispered, "A text message."

"Did you say a text message?"

"Yes, and it wasn't my fault. I'd been getting fake text

messages asking for money. One appeared to be sent by our neighbor. It read:

"Hi: This is Mary. My car's transmission needs repair. They won't accept American Express. Please help."

"Lots of establishments no longer accept American Express. So, I sent her my credit card number and security pin. It was a scam. Right then and there, I vowed never again to respond to one of those phony texts."

"I still don't see the connection, Elmo," said Max.

"A few days later, I got a text from Sylvia. She seldom texts. Her thing is Words With Friends."

"What happened?" Max urged.

The text read:

"My GPS sent me down a dirt road. Car out of gas. Poor signal. Please help."

"And you thought the text was bogus, right?"

Elmo nodded in agreement.

"That's understandable," said Max.

"Sylvia told me she was driving to an ashram in Charlotte. Suspicion crept in. Can you blame me?"

Elmo's complexion was turning red. His hands trembled. "I told myself, 'I'm not falling for this one.' Sadly, there's an exception to every rule, as my dad used to say."

"Tell me you didn't ignore the call," I said with an expression of disbelief.

Elmo slapped the palm of his hand against his head. "It wasn't a crank call. A trooper found her while answering a complaint about an abandoned car. It was Sylvia."

"Holy smokes, Elmo. And what happened then?"

"I apologized. I offered to buy more jewelry. Does it matter?"

"Of course, it does. We care about you," I insisted.

Elmo took a deep breath and let it out. "Sylvia packed up

and ran off to India with her yoga guru. She left the kids and me. It was a long time before I heard from her."

"Not a word?" asked Max.

"No. Sylvia divorced me."

❊ ❊ ❊

Six months after the divorce became final, I was struggling. I still coudn't operate the washing machine."

"What did you do?" asked Max.

"Hold on, Max. This conversation appears to be painful for Elmo."

"What could I do? First, I canceled Sylvia's cell phone and credit cards. Then with the children's best interest at heart, I married the au pair. Another mistake."

"Elmo, this is a complicated story," I said.

Elmo looked so sad. Nevertheless, his sincerity made me feel uncomfortable.

"It's all my fault. It all started years before at that ashram in the Berkshires. I suspected the guru was screwing Sylvia."

Elmo told us the story before. Nevertheless, I listened intently. I was intrigued by Elmo's ability to recall the finer details.

Elmo bit his lip. "I was angry. It was the first time I took a passionate stand."

"Nothing hurts more than when someone you love does something that causes you pain," I said.

"What happened next?" asked Max.

"I could hear Sylvia whimpering. And then the phone went silent."

❊ ❊ ❊

"About a month later, I was sipping a Teaser-size cappuccino when a repentant Sylvia called me collect from

India. She wanted to come home."

"Life has its ups and downs," Max said.

"It was too late. What choice did I have?"

"That was a long time ago," I added.

"Things got worse. My kids needed an au pair. I found one. She was twenty-five."

"How old were your children at the time?" Max asked.

"Nineteen and twenty," Elmo replied.

"Surely you're joking," I said with a laugh.

"Elmo, you told us your second wife was dead."

"I'm sorry, Max. The real story is embarrassing and infuriates me. I told you that I only lie when I need arises."

* * *

"The au pair divorced me. It all started at the corporate Christmas party. She wore a voluptuous outfit. I caught her flashing her boobs at one of the young guys standing at the bar. It happened so quickly. They scurried away before I could say lickety-split."

"What do you mean?" asked Max.

"She didn't come home that night. How could she treat me so shabbily? I paid for her new boobs, a car, the clothes, and drama school tuition."

"Elmo, you sure have a complicated life," I said.

"Oops, here come the twins, Dawn, and Deidre," Elmo said, gawking at the irresistible twenty-four-year-old Skipper sisters. Instantly, Elmo's demeanor changed. He picked up his unfinished coffee. "Excuse me, gentlemen. The Double D's are in the house. Their very presence is like an aphrodisiac. You know what they say at Jugz."

"Tell me," I said.

"Suspense is half the fun," Elmo blurted. He nearly tripped over a chair.

❋ ❋ ❋

Wouldn't it be wonderful to have a life-size instant replay of happier times to get us through the ugly ones?
Max Trottter

CHAPTER SIXTEEN

"A Surprise Revelation."

Breakfast at Jugz.

I worked late into the evenings after closing time. I knew that Sandra was doing my share of managing the store. Still, I was becoming obsessed with finishing Max's faux memoir.

Yet, another subject intrigued me - Evette, Elmo's second wife. I turned to the Internet to review newspaper files. I discovered a revelation. The headline read: "Au Pair Convicted."

"Elmo's second wife, Evette, wasn't dead. She had been the focus of a scandal. According to *The Post*, Evette French was found guilty of involuntary manslaughter.

The following day over breakfast at Jugz, I confronted Elmo. "Your child bride did three years probation, involuntary manslaughter, for drowning her lover in a jacuzzi. Was that the guy from the Christmas party?"

"Yes, that's true. But it was an accident, Matt."

"Why did you tell me Evette was dead?"

Elmo shrugged. "I don't know."

"Sure you do," I replied with a cryptic smile.

"Evette made me happy. She didn't kill her lover. It was an accidental erotic asphyxiation."

I caught myself nervously running my fingers through my hair. "You baffle me, Elmo. Have it your way. How could anyone find pleasure having an orgasm while having their head held underwater?"

Elmo stepped back. "Matt you are making me feel uncomfortable. And what would you know about it?"

"You can bet your ass that I'm not into it. It's a bizarre way to express love."

I watched Max slip his hands into his pants pockets and walk toward Jugz's boardwalk atrium. I sensed he wanted no part of this conversation. He never uttered a word He watched us from a distance.

Elmo glanced at a poker faced Max and back at me and said, "Whatever. You know little about me. Who are you to judge? Every man is entitled to his illusion. You're no award winning Pulitzer winner." Elmo's voice grew louder with the increased tension.

"Hold on Elmo. This doesn't have to be a shouting match. I was searching for a simple answer. I want to avoid including an unsubstantiated story in Max's memoir. I'm not sure Max should include events about Evette's affair."

"So, you are going to make a federal case out of this?"

"No, but here's my perspective, something is odd. You're the wealthiest man I know. You go on exotic vacations. You own a 1953 Buick, and huge home. And you are still unhappy. Can't you be satisfied with a woman's touch or the whisper of 'I love you?'"

* * *

Elmo pushed away from the table and shot back with a sudden anger. "Unlike you I don't have to ask a woman, - 'Do you love me?' - only to hear her reply, 'You know I do.' And that's no illusion. Matt *how do you* hold on without a woman's warm affectionate touch?"

Elmo's question hit me like one of Joe Palooka's left

hooks. He was right-on. I did long for the warm affectionate touch of a woman. Then, I thought of Sandra.

We are friends. Sandra and I seemed to have reached a mutual understanding. I don't want casual sex to alter the relationship.

CHAPTER SEVENTEEN

"Fiction or Reality?"

It's time we spice up the story. One day Max presented me with a challenge. He asked me to create a character for his faux memoir.

"Why, Max? Haven't I embellished enough?" I asked.

"True, but you make me out to be a plebeian. With all the beautiful women in your stories, where's mine?" asked Max.

"Max, it's your memoir. I can create a character. But let me warn you, once the character steps on to the page, the writing process involves emotional state of mind - happiness, love, fear and even shame. It's tougher than you seem to think."

"I need companionship in my life," Max replied.

"Max, it's easy to get trapped in the portal between fiction and reality, especially when it comes to romance."

"Please, Matt. Sex is no longer the priority."

"What the hell does than mean?"

"Matt, listening to Elmo talk about his love life, I feel left out. Promise me, not a word to Elmo."

"Max, what do you want from me?"

"I'm lonely. Please. Be a buddy. You're sitting in front of the computer. Grab a character worksheet and fashion someone special for me."

"It takes time, Max. Especially when it comes to women. I find them more complex then men. You not describing the so-called everyday girl, if there is such a woman."

"Want to know a secret?" Max asked.

"What secret, Max?"

"Dawn Skipper has a crush on you."

I was stunned. "The Double D's are too young for me. I'd feel awkward. Men are always eyeing that pair," I said.

"And some women, too. I'll bet Dawn is a ferocious lover, Matt," Max replied and winked.

"I'm not into a relationships, Max. I could be the Skipper sisters' grandfather."

Max shook his head in disapproval and laughed.

"Let's get back to your request, Max. You're asking me to write a narrative about a woman who doesn't exist?"

"Yes! Fix me up with an adventurous woman; five feet two inches, deep green eyes, chestnut hair, and suntanned body. A woman who adores me."

"Sounds like you've put a lot of thought into the character, Max."

"I have. She must be intelligent. I find intelligence attractive. Give her sexy spectacles too. The innocent appearance is so appealing. When Ann gets angry she takes off her glasses. My god, she looks so cute."

"Spectacles? In other words, you want her to be on the nerdy side?"

"No, I just want her to be attracted to a nerd - me."

"Of course you do." *Max you're such a geek.*

Then with a smile Max said. "I've saved the best for last. I've been dreaming about her. I know her name, too."

"Great. Tell me."

"Laura," replied the google-eyed Max. "Her name is Laura."

"I'll give it my best, Max. But promise me you'll go home an take a long cold shower."

CHAPTER EIGHTEEN

"The Reality of Love."

I struggled with Max's request to ease the hole in his heart. I recalled my own loneliness when Liz and I were no longer a couple. Is there a pivotal waypoint on our life journeys? A point in time when we determine - "Here is where it began or it came to an end?"

I ruminate excessively. At those times my inner critic - the inner voice that torments and reminds me - *"Matt, I own your heart."*

* * *

I vividly recall one evening, when I tried sharing my feelings with Liz. *Loneliness and sadness cast their shadows over me.*

I fumbled with my thoughts and the corkscrew while opening a bottle of pino grigio awaiting Liz's response.

She glanced at me and grimaced. "Matt, is this going to be a good story or a bad one? You always tell sad stories about your childhood."

It was a rare moment of truth, a dissident chord.

I considered Liz the narrator of *my* journey. Truth can be cruel. *Move on. My childhood does have too many secrets.*

My circle of friends seemed to be growing smaller by the month. Absent my fellow dreamers with whom to share my hopes and bucket list adventures. I was becoming dangerously nostalgic.

I looked into Liz's deep blue eyes. They never lied. Her eyes revealed how mediocre and boring I had become.

I sipped my wine hoping to avoid that reality. *Just once can we find a way to make the evening turn out right?* Our struggling marriage was nearing an end.

Enough about me. Let's return to Max Trotter's feelings of loneliness. I find it fascinating, even mind-boggling, how a fictional character's role becomes more lifelike than I initially imagined. The character leaves the worksheet profile, steps on to the manuscript page, and - abracadabra - the character comes alive and takes control of the storyline. My only alternative is the delete key.

Adding the final touches to Laura's background and fitting her into the memoir took longer than expected.

"Max, how can you be certain that you are real?" I asked.

"I'm real, Matt. My conscience tells me so."

Recently, I read a quote from *The Velveteen Rabbit* - "Once you are real you can't become unreal again. It lasts for always."

Max subscribes to Elmo's contention that everyone is entitled to their illusion. I suspect that Max is deceiving himself. Reality can be painful.

❋ ❋ ❋

"Love like reality is often elusive and painful. Love can be a magical healing elixir? Still, love like magic is often an illusion.

Javan

CHAPTER NINETEEN

"Meet The Amazing Laura Finley."

Max and Ann agreed to a legal seperation. Most weeknights found Max at Jugz with Elmo and the twins, but he played golf on the weekends. Rain or shine, Max was a regular at the Grille, sipping a Ketel One martini straight up with three olives. That's when Laura Finley came on the scene.

From time to time a band performed at the Grille. On this Friday evening the bar was crowded and Max searched the room for an empty seat. The band was on a break. Max spied Josie MCarthy, an acquaintance sitting at a corner table with another woman. Josie sang with the band. Josie smiled and waved Max to their table.

"Hi Max. Where is Ann?" Josie asked as if she hadn't heard of Max's seperation. There are no secrets in Deepmarsh Village.

"Ann isn't with me, tonight."

"Please, join us. This is my friend, Laura Finley. Laura just moved to the Strand. We played golf today. Laura this is Max Trotter."

And that's how it all began.

* * *

Laura smiled. Max momentarily froze. The bespectacled Laura with chestnut hair, deep dark green eyes, and tanned complexion captivated Max. *Déjà vu? Incredible. It feels like Laura stepped out of my dreams.*

"Have we met before, Ms. Finley?"

"I don't believe so."

"Of course not. I certainly would have remembered," Max replied. Max can be awkward in social situations.

Laura reacted with flirtatious smile that made her look even more attractive.

It all happened so innocently. Doesn't it always? Laura Finley was years younger and divorced. Max felt magically younger, too. Nevertheless, the two became immersed in a conversation about music.

Later, Max told me, "Matt, I am still a bit fuzzy about how she walked into my life. Being with Laura is a daydream. I'm convinced Laura was created just for me."

I smiled knowingly. Then I broke the news.

I whispered, "Surprise, Max. As you requested, I created the woman of your dreams, Laura Finley. Laura is a loving, and light-hearted. You'll soon discover that she tastes like French toast smothered in butter and real maple syrup."

I still needed to tweak Laura's backstory. I withheld my one trepidation. Laura Finley, possessed all the physical endowments Max wished for. Nonetheless, Laura Finley is a person in her own right. I hope Laura doesn't break Max's heart. *Tread lightly, Max.*

❉ ❉ ❉

Their relationship evolved at a casual pace. Weeks later, they had not moved to the "next step," which didn't trouble Max. He was in no rush.

Max shared his feelings of uneasiness with me.

"Here's the rub, Matt. Fairden is a small town. I still feel awkward when I run into Ann especially when I'm with

Laura. After all, Ann and I are still married."

"Max, I must confess that I too feel angst when I meet Liz. Being friendly doesn't mean sharing a friendship. Instead, we have a particular time in our lives that calls for treating people courteously. And that doesn't come easy. You and I share another trait, Max."

"And what's that?"

"We both have a strong need for validation. Some call it the crybaby complaint. After years of marriage, I wanted to hear that I was lovable. Liz no longer felt that way."

Max shrugged and said, "I guess."

* * *

One evening, Max and Laura sat at a table in the far corner of the Grille.

Laura said, "Max, I'm the one who is always taking the initiative. I'd appreciate you calling me occasionally. Moving our relationship up a notch doesn't mean we are sleeping together, or does it?"

"I don't know," Max murmured.

"Max. It's all quite innocent. You know it. What's troubling you?"

"It's awkward. Ann still lives in Deepmarsh."

"By now, she knows you are seeing someone. She doesn't know the extent of it. Would you rather we stopped seeing each other?"

"Of course not," he quickly responded. "It's complicated. What will the kids think?"

"It's up to you, Max. Your children are approaching retirement age. My kids are out of college and on their own. Life is short. So, please sleep on it."

Max sure knew how to pick his women. Laura didn't side-step something she felt important. In addition to her abundant qualities, Laura Finley possessed courage and congruity.

"Give me a call. Max, you treat our relationship like I'm a fictional character in a love story. Face it. Being real can be painful for both of us. I'm leaving it up to you. Call or don't call. Either way I'll understand. Incidentally, it's your turn to pick up the tab." Laura touched Max's hand and abruptly walked away.

Why didn't I go after her? Maxed watched a couple of the men at the bar eye Laura as she left the grille. Laura is a head turner. She's too good to be true. How could I let her walk away?

From a woke point of view Max is superficial. But Laura does have a great figure. Max is shallow, but when you're right, you're right.

✳ ✳ ✳

Max called Laura the following day. They agreed to meet at Lombardi's that evening. It's at a small quiet place on the Bypass, a distance from Deepmarsh Village.

Max nervously worked his way through the garlic knots when the inevitable happened.

"Max, how about coming back to my place after this?" Laura asked.

He dropped the garlic knot in surprise. His face flushed.

"Wow. Isn't that what I'm supposed to ask?"

"No Max. I have the option, also."

"In the movies, they get around to the intimacies while sipping the last drops of wine. I haven't finished the garlic knots."

"Max, you are incorrigible," Laura replied. "I'm not bragging, but I suspect more than one man in Deepmarsh Village would relish that proposal."

Max leaned over the table and whispered, "Forgive me, Laura, but there's something you should know."

Laura smiled and interrupted before Max could finish sharing his secret. "Max, how old are you? No, don't tell me. I'll put it another way. We are adults, Max, or we're supposed to be. I'm inviting you back to my condo for coffee."

"Simple as that?" Max asked.

"And uncomplicated. I promise," said Laura.

Max nervously stuffed a garlic knot in his mouth.

"Max, don't be so anxious. Everything will be alright," Laura assured him.

No need for the details. Max stayed the night.

* * *

Nearly four days passed. Max left two more messages on Laura's answering machine and one on her cell phone. She didn't return the calls.

When the phone eventually rang, it was Elmo.

"I called you a half dozen times the other night. Is something wrong?" he asked.

"No. Everything is great," Max said.

"Of course. I suspect you slept with that delicious Laura Finley."

"Elmo, my love life is none of your business."

"You have me all wrong, Max. I wasn't asking about your sex life. Hanky-panky for the aging is not without problems, including increased risk for sexually transmitted diseases."

"Thanks, Elmo. What do you want?"

"Max, I'm only trying to be friendly."

"Nonsense, Elmo. You are probing. One last time Elmo, what's up?"

"Are you still stuck on Laura?"

"I like her, but Laura hasn't returned my calls. So, I've stopped calling."

"Don't be embarrassed, Max. You experienced a male age-appropriate sexual malfunction. Right? That's why you aren't talking. Protocol demands you share that information with the lady well in advance."

"Don't go there, Elmo."

"Hold on, Max. Take it from me. Either you'll never hear from her again, or she'll call and remind you that the next time bring your blue pills."

Max grew silent. *I'm sick of the blue pill jokes.*

"Elmo you've stepped over the line."

Elmo mastered the art of diverting the conversation. He was quick with emotional deflection, too. It's an art that only comes with a lifetime of practice. Here it comes. The segue wasn't a surprise.

"Let's get together and discuss your garage band."

"A garage band is the furthest thing from my mind."

Max was too preoccupied to think about a garage band. His attempt to keep a low-key relationship with Laura seemed overwhelming.

"Thanks for the call, Elmo."

Max overthinks, and that's a predicament. Why is making something simple so difficult?

Perhaps the answer lies in knowing how to be in the moment.

❋ ❋ ❋

"If you could relive a year in your life, what age would you choose?"

Deidre Skipper

CHAPTER TWENTY

"Get Back, Loretta"

This may be the time to take a breather from the woes of Max's love life, and garage band befuddlement to explore a little known side of his personality. Max has several triggers that set him off and Elmo knows all of them.

Elmo invited me to join Max and the Double D's for a coffee. When I arrived the gang was sipping 16-ounce Naughties, black with Jugz Double Shots served in double walled espresso glasses reserved for Elmo and his guests.

"None for me, thanks. I'm driving. I'll have a Teaser." *I begged-off. Elmo's Double Shot concoction is the closest thing to a double Mary Jane Gummy Bear.*

Dawn whispered, "I'll get it for you Matt. Max and Elmo are on a roll. Please don't egg him on." Dawn's pat on my butt, as I sat down, caught me by surprise.

Max said, "I'm not a fan of discussing religion, politics or complaints about erectile dysfunction, especially in **mixed** company, but I need some advice. I'm up ten times at night taking a leak. I'm exhausted."

"Had your prostate checked?" I asked.

"Not me buddy," Max replied.

"Maybe I'm wrong, but that's why some guys die from prostate cancer. It isn't macho to share the 'news,'" I added.

"Every year, professional football teams wear pink cleats to support breast cancer awareness. I could be wrong, but I don't recall blue football cleats giving a shout-out for prostate cancer awareness," Elmo said.

I nodded in agreement. "For my money, the digital exam is the best way to go."

"Stop. Let's move on," said Max.

"Wow! You guys are squeamish when it come to discussing your bodies," said Deidre.

Max's complexion was turning gray. I tried to figure out the look on his face. Was it from disgust or fear?

"The digital exam turns me off. But your right, Matt. And I'm fixin' to go." he said.

"I think the country is going mad," Deidre exclaimed . "You gray-haired old men huddle in dark corners bragging about you penis sizes while you're making rules for how women should live their lives. You old farts make laws that control our bodies, but you can't control our our sexuality and our dreams, at least not mine."

"Holy smokes, Elmo. What are you feeding this girl?" Max asked in jest.

"I'm serious, Max," said Deidre. "It's no joke. We're getting into election time and the country is at war with itself. The bullshit TV ads are frightening. Politicians give speeches about protecting children from harrowing history. Then Bingo! They spend millions of dollars to promote adult fear campaigns. Kids watch TV, too. It's madness. It's open season on the vulnerable. They make good targets. Well, I fight like a woman. And I'm getting ready to kick ass." Deidre pushed away from the table and walked outside.

I was stunned. This was a side of the daunting Deidre I had never seen.

"What the hell was that all about?" Max asked. "Something I said?"

Just then Dawn returned with my coffee. "Where's Deidre going?" Dawn asked.

"She wanted some fresh air," I said.

Dawn sat down. She looked troubled. "Deidre is too serious these days. We feel Big Brother is watching our every move," Dawn added.

Dawn's remark silenced our conversation. I don't know where our country is headed, but I want to believe there's more to it than sex.

Suddenly, Elmo pounded the table. "Big Brother. That's all Deidre talks about these days. She forced me to put tape over the camera lenses on my TV. Siri and Alexa are banned from my love nest."

"I read the novel, *1984*," Dawn replied.

"You're reading novels, too?" Elmo asked.

"Yes Daddy. Deidre told me to read *1984*. Lately, you've been taking a lot of naps. Deidre convinced me that everything boils down to money and sex."

Max' fingers tapped the table as he grew increasingly agitated. "What's happening to the twins? Which brings me back to my point," Elmo asserted.

✻ ✻ ✻

"What was your point, Elmo?" I asked.

"The whole country has run amuck. Politicians need term limits, especially in Washington. They get into office, and refuse to leave. If they lose an election, they fight in court. When all that fails - they become lobbyists. It's a revolving door." Max was on a roll.

"I think you're exaggerating to prove a point, Max," I said. "There are honest politicians on both sides of the aisle. We don't hear about them. Bad times demand bad news. Somebody has to step up and take responsibility - good news and bad. But no. All I seem to see and read are the back row howlers."

Then Elmo said, "I watched those culprits wreck the Capitol." Elmo's face turned bright red. They have some balls calling the attack on our Capitol a 'legitimate political discourse. And it sure wasn't mostly peaceful chaos."

"And they sure as hell were not taking a tour. That is the best politically correct description I've ever heard. Beats 'plausible deniability,' the shabbby CIA term for contesting responsibility," replied Max.

"It was a despicable example of public life. I heard a guy on television say the whole thing was a hoax. Honestly, not much I can do about it," I conceded. "That's his opinion and he makes sure he isn't stating a fact."

"Please don't preface your remarks with 'honestly.' That's woke."

Max said, "I stopped watching prime-time news. All you get is ten minutes of Washington antics and ten minutes of lies. The remaining time is devoted to pharmaceutical ads."

"I agree. The same folks who control the pharmaceutical industry sponsor prime-time broadcast news," said Elmo.

I cringed. "That sounds too conspiratorial. Tell me it isn't so."

Max piped-up. "I stopped watching for a practical reason. I discovered if I didn't have a particular illness when the broadcast began, I had it when the program ended. What crap. 'Ask your doctor if this drug is right for you.'"

Max glanced at the Skipper twins. They wanted no part of the discussion.

 Out of the blue Max asked Elmo, "What happened to the two-bathtubs Cialis ad?"

Elmo responded, "I asked my doctor the same question. And he told me, 'It is what it is.'"

Dawn sat opposite me. She joined Max nervously tapping her nails on the table. I could tell from her facial expression she was exasperated. "Where is this conversation headed?" she asked.

I shrugged.

* * *

"So Max, answer Dawn's question. What's this conversation about?" I asked.

"Simple. I think the power brokers, and the politicians, aren't getting enough sex, " Max replied.

I gave Max a quizzical look. "Sex again?"

"Yes, sex," Max insisted.

Elmo added, "Sylvia claims that sex is my cure-all. She's right."

"Good for you," Max exclaimed. "If I ran for office, my slogan would promise 'an orgasmatron in every pocket.' I think the government should pay for an erotic chip implant by golly."

I asked, "Max, what's an orgasmatron? Was it invented by the Pentagon? No. Still, with all the distrust circulating, I'd be careful talking about chip implants. Sounds like another conspiracy theory."

"We know," said Dawn while looking at Deidre to nod in agreement. You gotta read *1984.*

"I never read that book, but they say the Chinese stole the US mini-chip-prototype," said Max. "I heard you can purchase one on the grey market. It's rumored they are manufactured in Monaco. Pocket-size stimulators have a short battery life. Still, press the buttom and - WHAM!" Max's arms shot above his head as though he was about to explode."

"Here comes the punchline," I said.

Max laughed. People get greedy and the chip runs out of juice. Who wants the battery to fail just before they peak?"

"Hopefully, with an improved chip the battery will last longer," I said. "Besides, I read that a team of scientists in Denmark have invented an internal generator."

"Thank god. Can't count on Zuckerberg. The world needs the stimulator chip now," I said.

"For heaven's sake, Matt. There's a world-wide chip shortage. Toyota is buying them up," Elmo said.

"Elmo, I hope they purchase the right chip." said Dawn. The rest of us looked at each other in surprise.

Naturally, Elmo carried the concept one step further. "Imagine the implant with an on-call hologram. I'll bet on the hologram," he quipped."I'm joking."

"I can't imagine having sex with a three-dimensional image. Who wants to wear those awkward glasses?" Max asked.

"You mean those awkward goggles? How do they fit over glasses?" I asked.

"Beats me,"Max replied. "Hey, is 'beats me a no-no term?

Just then Dawn said, "Daddy this conversation is rediculous. We're headed home."

I agreed with Dawn. Time to head home. I get lonely at times, but I'm not into a hologram lover.

"Don't leave," Max insisted.

✻ ✻ ✻

Once the ladies departed, Max returned to the orgasmatron. "A low-cost orgasmatron might promote world peace. Make love – Not war!" Max said.

I replied, "Max, lighten up. Are you losing your sense of humor? The orgasmatron is a dream. Please stop. Your fulmination is drawing attention."

By the way, the pill is going generic," said Max added.

"I know. But companies are trying to put the kibosh on generic up-starts," said Elmo.

Max shook his head. "I get so frustrated. I just want to howl."

"Calm down, Max." Elmo the old fox, eyed two women eavesdropping at a nearby table.

"Matt, get a load of the one wearing the open-toed stilettos. Do you think those Capri pants destroy the look?" Elmo asked with a smile.

I whispered, "Nada. But I'm warning you. By implication your comment crosses the so-called politically incorrect line in the sand."

"No one pays attention to any lines," Max said.

"I don't give a rat's ass about the niceties of social protocol," Elmo grumbled. "Ms. Stilettos looks fit and her friend is quite nice, also."

"I'll bet Ms. Stilettos does Pilates," I responded in her defense.

Ms. Stilettos smiled. Elmo earned a black belt in flirtatious eye contact.

"Excuse me, gentlemen. It's time for a refill." Elmo moved in for the kill.

Ms. Stilettos caught Elmo's attention with another intriguing but shameless smile. As Elmo walked to the counter for a refill, Miss Stilettos reached out and brushed his arm.

"Amen about the chip, my friend," Ms. Stilettos whispered. "My gentleman friend needs something. I lay there with my eyes closed wishing and hoping, but the creek don't rise. I have my needs, too."

CHAPTER TWENTY-ONE

"Stay For the Night."

E nter Matt Nagle.Let's pause here. By now, you've caught on. Elmo is an eccentric with a passion for investments and women. The Skipper twins sweet-talked Max into opening the Salon de Beauté a few doors away from Emma's Bookstore. Sometimes the twins' behavior leads people to underestimate them.

We visited Elmo's boardwalk café earlier. I thought you might enjoy Jugz's backstory nonetheless. It all started about a year ago at the grand opening of Emma's Bookstore. Ben Elder, Fairden's mayor at the time, announced Elmo's latest endeavor, Jugzjava.com.

Elder spotted the diminutive Elmo French in the crowd during the ribbon-cutting and abruptly shouted for Elmo to join him. Elmo declined. Nevertheless, Elmo's two companions, the shapely Skipper twins, Dawn, and Deidre, pushed their way through the crowd and gave Elder several "big-daddy" hugs.

The twins, sported scanty two-piece workout ensembles, sure to be gym influencers.

Embroided across their sports bras was Jugz's logo and tag line. The Mayor stood back and squinted to read the delicate embroidery: "Lip-Smacking – when you feel like it."

Elder, the obnoxious sloth, grabbed Deidre, spun her around with his hooked, claw-like hands, and bellowed, "Folks, Elmo French has plans to open Jugzjava.com, a boardwalk café around the corner from his salon."

Then Elder pointed at Deidre's sports bra and exclaimed, "Elmo , you are a marketing genius." Elder unceremoniously patted the twins on the butt and sent the Double D's scurrying back to Elmo. The crowd roared. And that was that.

Emma, the bookstore's owner, later remarked, "Elder, that son of a bitch, probably staged the whole damn thing."

✻ ✻ ✻

Elmo earned a reputation for being an intelligent speculator and a smooth operator. Elmo wanted a significant role in Fairden's growth. And here is where the plot thickens.

The villainous Mayor Elder was subsequently indicted for bank fraud. In return for fingering his cohorts, Elder plead guilty to lesser crimes. Ben Elder is serving time in Otisville Federal Prison Camp, the "cushiest prison" in the system.

Elmo never missed an opportunity to exploit a situation. Succinctly put, Elmo was sleeping with Elder's neglected wife. It all started with dinner at the Freeport Hotel Grille.

Following two dirty martinis and several dozen clams on the half-shell, Mrs. Elder presented an opportunity Elmo could not refuse.

The lonely Gladys Elder suspected Elmo's ulterior intentions. Still, the breathless woman threw herself at his mercy with ecstasy and abandonment.

"Elmo, come home with me. Stay the night," Gladys pleaded.

Through a night of unbridled eroticism, Elmo weaseled his way into Gladys every nook, niche, and cranny thanks to those clams.

He callously captured her heart. By dawn, the helpless

Gladys innocently exposed her soul, too.

Then Elmo pounced. "Tell me, Gladys, what was your crooked husband's next financial scam?"

"The abandoned building on the corner of the boardwalk. A foreclosure," she moaned. "It's a steal."

Gladys awakened to find her lover gone.

Elmo purchased the building and ungraciously discarded Mrs. Elder.

❋ ❋ ❋

Elmo, the keen-eyed entrepreneur, savored what many greedy coffee shops poured down the drain; an affordable cup of coffee, the local newspaper, and a neighborly conversation. A reputation Jugz would build upon.

❋ ❋ ❋

"In my youth, I, too, entertained some illusions, but I soon recovered from them."

Bill D. Moyers

CHAPTER TWENTY-TWO

"Words With Friends and Anonymous People, Too."

One morning Elmo met Max and me on the boardwalk. "Hey buddy you're late. What's up?" Max asked. Elmo's wrinkled pants and tattered sweat shirt were out of character for our dapper friend. As we walked toward the Jugz café, Elmo told us something unexpected.

"I want my marriage to work this time. Yet, everything is going haywire." My friend sounded sad and on the verge of crying.

"Elmo, have you thought about why you remarried Sylvia? After all, Sylvia is now, and forever will be Sylvia," Max asked.

"I blame myself. I'm always doing something wrong to anger Sylvia. Oh well, I guess it's part of growing older."

"The last few times we were together, you seemed a little down," I said.

"I'm blind when it comes to Sylvia. When she lets her black-laced nightgown slip to the floor and whispers, 'Come on, baby, light my fire,' I'm putty in her hands."

"Elmo, perhaps you're trying too hard. Your home is a mansion. From what I've seen, you have tried your best. Sylvia's engagement ring could choke a horse. You own a 1953 Buick Super. In spite of what preceded you still remarried Sylvia," I said.

"Matt's right. My god Elmo, how many guys remarry their first wife?" Max asked.

"I looked it up. Fifteen percent of divorced couples remarry each other. I realized that I still loved Sylvia," Elmo sighed. "We were comfortable for a while. No pretense. And the sex was wonderful! Then Sylvia started to change. When we talked, it was like Sylvia wasn't there. She wouldn't come to bed until midnight. Max, what do you know about *Words With Friends*?"

"The computer word game?" Max asked.

"Your faceless opponent can be a friend or a stranger. Why would Sylvia want to play a video game with a stranger?" I asked.

"That seems dangerous to me. Imagine someone getting it off while playing a video game with Sylvia?" Max asked.

I scowled at Max. I sensed from Elmo's expression that Max's comment hurt Elmo's feelings. Having said that, I've heard a lot of folks are into it.

"Sylvia's gone over the edge. We rarely speak with one another. When I say, 'pass the remote,' Sylvia glares. She shushes me and continues playing. I'm amazed how she can watch TV and play *Words With Friends* at the same time."

"Elmo it sounds like things aren't going well," I said.

"I swear it's worse," he remarked, looking out over the river.

I said, "I'm sorry, Elmo. Maybe you should see a therapist. Would Sylvia agree to marriage counseling?"

"No. Not again. Sylvia insists everything's okay. It isn't. I'm frustrated and unhappy."

"How about going on your own?" I asked.

"I tried," he replied. "It didn't work for me."

I was hesitant to reveal that I had gone through a period of depression, even to a friend. You can share you have hemorrhoids. Don't tell them you are in counseling.

"I'm upping my Valium to 10 milligrams," Elmo said.

"Shouldn't you talk with your doctor, first?" Max asked.

"No. I'll be careful."

Arriving at Jugz, Elmo ordered his usual 16-ounce

Naughty which he sips, but never finishes. I had the 12-ounce Sassy mocha. I don't recall Max's order.

"Maybe Sylvia is going through the 'change of life.' I recall Ann's hot flashes," said Max.

I bit my tongue fearing my comment might expose me to Deepmarsh gossip. The mention of Liz's hot flashes was on her "Do Not Discuss" list.

* * *

I finished my Sassy and ordered an apple fritter. "Elmo, what would you do if you knew what to do?" I asked.

He gave me a suspicious look. I rephrased the question. "Did you ever think about where you've been and where you are going, Elmo?"

"Not really, Matt. I'm in my seventies. I'm struggling with where I am. I'm broken-hearted. We never raised our voices. Sylvia and I were close. We always playfully whispered. Now we are at a distance. We even shout in bed."

Elmo's hands trembled; a dead give-away he was in trouble. I recognized the signs.

I looked at my phone. Sandra was expecting me to meet a vendor at Emma's Bookstore.

"Gentlemen, I have to leave. Back to the salt mines and editing Max's manuscript. Elmo, I'm usually around over the weekends, if you want to talk. Give me a call first, so I know you're coming."

CHAPTER TWENTY-THREE

"An Intervention"

A week passed. I wondered how Elmo French was faring. He seemed to be avoiding Max and me. Undoubtedly something we said. I invited Max and Elmo for a glass of wine at Emma's Bookstore after we closed. "Why don't you guys browse the bookshelves while I open the wine?"

Max was sitting in my favorite worn leather chair when I returned. He was flipping a book's pages.

"This book caught my eye. I thought Elmo might read it," said Max as he handed me the paperback. I smiled. "*101 PLACES NOT TO REVISIT*? Surely, you're joking."

"No. It might be an icebreaker. Something like 'Here's another place not to revisit - your ex-wife."

"Max, I was hoping our get-together might cheer him, not make him unhappier."

Just then, Elmo joined us. "Show Elmo the book," Max insisted.

"No thanks." I tossed it on the counter.

"Sounds like a self-help book to me," Elmo said.

"Exactly Elmo! Write a book about Sylvia." Max laughed and rambled on oblivious to his friend's body language. Elmo sank deeper into his chair as though he was trying to hide.

"That book is about bum vacations. You could write about bum marriages," Max said.

"You can be a real shit, Max," Elmo shot back.

"I'm joshing you, Elmo."

"Then laugh at this. I can summarize your life as screwed-up shit. Your garage band is nothing more than a metaphor for a bum marriage; a journey with no destination," Elmo retorted, as he white-knuckled the chair.

I didn't want to get into the mix, but things were tense. Elmo's tense nervousness alarmed me. Nevertheless I said, "Perhaps it might be helpful if we stopped talking about Sylvia and our own personal problems and listened to Elmo."

"Great idea," grumbled Elmo.

Max appeared stumped.

I walked to my office and opened a bottle of pino noir. "Boys, let's relax and enjoy some wine. We need a break." I sat back and sipped my wine.

The wine didn't help. Elmo grew more intense. "My stomach aches. I'm starting to feel awful. Sylvia forces me to practice breathing while we are having sex in our love tubs. How could anyone find pleasure in sex while holding their breath underwater?" asked Elmo. "Sylvia claims it reduces performance pressure and focuses on pleasure. It relieved tension."

"Sounds hedonistic," said Max. He gave Elmo a "good old boy" punch on the arm and a "thumbs-up."

Elmo's body jerked as though Max had interrupted a visceral experience.

"Max what the hell was that for? Boys, if you think this conversation is cheering me up, you're crazy," said Elmo.

I felt his angst.

"You guys make me feel worse than the first time Sylvia threatened to leave. I don't want to revisit that place. Never! No more divorces," Elmo proclaimed like a fish gasping for air.

"Are you okay, Elmo?" Max asked.

"I need a breath of fresh air." Elmo pushed himself out of the leather chair and walked to the back entrance and onto the patio. He never returned.

We didn't resolve a thing for Elmo. No doubt we made matters worse.

* * *

"You always learn more from failure
than success. Adversity is the great teacher."
Linda Ronstadt.

CHAPTER TWENTY-FOUR

"Your Advice Isn't Helping."

Matt and Max realized that their well-intentioned intervention with Elmo failed. It was about two in the morning when Max's phone rang. It was Elmo

"How are you, Elmo?" Max asked.

"Okay, I guess. Matt told me you made an appointment to see a shrink. Maybe I should see one, too."

"Elmo it's late. I need my sleep."

"Does she have possibilities?"

"Elmo why does everything have to be sexually motivated?"

"Because it does, Max. One way or the other."

"You told me to find a woman. I did."

"Good night, Elmo. We can talk about this in the morning. If it makes you feel better, I'm sorry I messed up and hurt your feelings the other evening at the bookstore."

✻ ✻ ✻

The following morning over coffee at Jugz, Elmo French preached his well-intentioned marriage platitudes.

"Seeing a shrink is serious business, Max. Granted it takes balls," Elmo said. "I can't go through it again."

"Elmo, that's the first compliment you ever gave me."

"It wasn't a compliment, Max. It's the truth. I told you, Sylvia and I tried it a couple of times. It was a disaster."

"Why?"

"When we arrived home after counseling, Sylvia would slap me in the back of the head and toss me to the ground."

"What?"

"Sylvia said I gave the counselor too much information. Our sex life was none of the guy's friggin' business."

"Aren't you supposed to talk about personal stuff?"Max asked.

"Not with Sylvia. Confidentially Max, I think Sylvia attended marriage counseling because her lawyer said it would look good for a divorce settlement."

❈ ❈ ❈

Mulling over recent events, I am reminded of saying attributed to Mark Twain. "What's the sense of wresting with a pig? You both get muddy and the pig enjoys it."

"Everybody has their opinion and justifies it -
no matter what!"
Anonymous

CHAPTER TWENTY-FIVE

"Meet Johnny Scrubbs."

Max Trotter's latest squeeze is Laura Finley. Johnny Scrubbs is Laura's half-brother. He is humble, submissive, and like most men, easily manipulated by a beautiful woman and Fireball. The first sips taste like heaven, but burn like hell. In fairness to Johnny, I'll allow our gridiron hero's backstory to unfold.

Coach Carr hired Johnny to paint the kitchen and run errands while Coach attended a football clinic in Syracuse. In Coach's absence, Jane Carr, the coach's former student and now his new wife, introduced the faultless boy to Winston cigarettes, vodka, and afternoon delight.

Coach suspected Jane's dalliance but he trusted Johnny, Fairden High School's varsity quarterback. The boy's innocence intrigued Jane. Johnny's energy was remarkable. And so, she determined to test his endurance. The hard-working boy deserved a reward.

Payday arrived one hot summer afternoon as Johnny was about to leave. Johnny blanched. Jane lifted the spaghetti straps of her bright summer dress and let it fall to the floor. Unlike his lone experiences, Jane awakened Johnny's dormant passion.

Jane slowly reached out and touched the lad. One might conclude Jane took advantage of the boy's naivete, but not for long. Johnny was a fast learner and coachable.

It was an unforgettable summer until the Skipper twins moved into town.

❊ ❊ ❊

The Back Story.

The elementary school-aged Skipper sisters moved from Patchogue to nearby Sayville, New York, where they lived for a time with their mother's sister, Beyrl, not Beryl, while their parents worked things out.

Mr. and Mrs. Skipper, Ernie and Constance, had fallen out of love.

It was a complex situation. Constance, a devout Catholic, declined a divorce. Ernie, a Protestant, was inclined towards celibacy after the shock of siring twins.

Aunt Beyrl lived in an apartment building halfway between the local elementary school and Main Street. She was a loving, bibulous woman who was unattached at the time but enjoyed the company of several gentlemen.

Aunt Beyrl was a night owl and a late sleeper. The obedient Dawn and Deidre would find two quarters on the kitchen table each morning before school. The twins were instructed to tiptoe down the apartment stairs and proceed directly to the corner stationery store. They would patiently sit at the soda fountain counter, waiting for their English muffins and a shared cup of coffee. Fifty cents was a bargain, but Aunt Beyrl had an understanding with the owner.

Twenty minutes later, the girls hurried out the door and headed home, but not before Deidre snatched a *Daily News* or *Daily Racing Form*.

Aunt Beyrl followed the news and the ponies.

❊ ❊ ❊

For the sake of the children, Ernie and Constance

decided to reunite following their prolonged separation.

Ernie and Constance rationalized it was best for the children. Long Island living was expensive, too. It was a pivotal decision for the loveless couple. I sympathize with Ernie and Constance. Many parents, not all, make personal sacrifices that their children fail to appreciate until a moment of truth, perhaps at a parent's eulogy.

A few months later, the Skipper family moved to Fairden, where Ernie found work as a mailman. (Oops! A postal worker.)

The Skipper twins joined the Fairden cheerleading squad.

Johnny and most of the football team turned to watch the girls run to the football fields' sideline for their first practice.

Bam! It was love at first sight. And that's how it all began for Johnny and the Skipper sisters.

* * *

The Double D's weren't into puppy love. Naturally, as with all things Skipper, there was one caveat. The sisters insisted Johnny "go steady." Back in the day, the arrangement implied exclusivity.

Deidre raged when Johnny gave Dawn his high school ring. Johnny purchased a second. Johnny had not yet experienced all sides of the Skipper sisters' personalities. The envious twins watched each other like vultures. And to paraphrase Herman Melville - God help thee old man...a vulture feeds upon the heart forever.

To Johnny's dismay, going steady also included a compulsory "ménage à trois" which suited the twins' appetites. Shy Johnny reluctantly agreed.

Ernie and Constance Skipper were at the movies on the designated Saturday evening.

Shazam!

Dawn and Deidre were incredible and determined beyond their years. Deidre was dark and deep while Dawn was light and fluffy. Welcome to Paradise.

The story of Johnny's first Saturday night with the Double D's still enhances the Skippers' mythology, and Johnny Scrubbs became a high school legend.

❋ ❋ ❋

The twins frequently squabbled. Most memorable was the catfight over Johnny's Fairden High School varsity sweater. The tiff started in the school cafeteria. It erupted the following Friday night at the Hillcrest Diner. The customers cheered as Johnny's prized varsity sweater was ripped to shreds along with the sisters' blouses.

Johnny was humiliated. The guys from the Varsity Club went bullshit. Someone called the cops. The disheveled twins rushed to Johnny's car, and the trio made their getaway. Johnny was pissed-off, but make-up sex at the marina eased the tension.

❋ ❋ ❋

After high school graduation, Johnny took a job as a cable installer. Then one evening, he proposed marriage. Dawn was for it, but Deidre balked.

"Mom and dad think you are a great guy, Johnny.

But polygamy is expensive. And daddy thinks that you need a better job before he agrees to giving you our hands in marriage. Something that can provide the lifestyle we deserve," Deidre insisted.

"Fairden is a small town, and people gossip. And there's something else we've been meaning to talk about," Deidre added.

"And what's that?" the perplexed Johnny asked.

"An open relationship. Johnny, lately you seem so tired. Afternoon delight! You've lost your endurance."

"But not my enthusiasm for a prolonged playtime," he argued. The twins shrugged. Dawn frowned and Deidre scowled.

An exhausted and disillusioned Johnny sank into a chair and said, "Ladies, I'm working my ass off to keep you in jewelry and designer clothes."

✿ ✿ ✿

Sadly, the twins were unresponsive. ""Johnny, we love you, but we have our needs. Johnny, you aren't tickling our sparkle," said Dawn.

The sisters' comments increased the psychological pressure on Johnny's libido. As hard as he tried, Johnny couldn't light the ladies' fire. Unfortunately, for Johnny, the Skipper twins couldn't or wouldn't accept that he didn't lack enthusiasm. He lacked stamina. Johnny was exhausted.

"Come on, Johnny, we've had a rough day," the twins pleaded. "We need to be re-energized."

For most lovers, a temporary physical default need not disable their love communication.

Like most men, Johnny struggled. He didn't realize as older men do that frequent malfunctions are part of owning a penis. The Skippers' sexual appetite intensified.

"If you don't improve your performance Johnny, we will have to swap you for a new stud," threatened the mean-spirited Deidre.

The loyal, love-struck, Johnny failed to read the writing on the wall.

CHAPTER TWENTY-SIX

"What He Did For Love."

The saga continues. Ever since their childhood days of snatching a newspaper from the stationery store, Deidre's game plans increased in size and daring. Deidre's lastest scheme - a duo street band, with Dawn on saxophone and Deidre on bass guitar - demonstrated an unusual resourcefulness and cleverness in execution.

The provocatively attired Skippers played 50's cover songs backed by pirated soundtracks. "Impulse," the Skippers' street band, was a hit. What they lacked in musical talent, they made up for in gyrations. On warm summer nights, Fairden's marina boardwalk bustled with tourists.

The sisters proved immensely popular. An encore filled the tip jar. That's when Deidre, the band's manager, turned to Dawn and said, "If we can make a bundle here, can you imagine how much more we will make this summer in Patchogue or Sayville? The Fire Island crowd tosses sensibilities and their money to the wind on their wild weekends, Deidre insisted.

Dawn and Deidre kissed Johnny goodbye and returned to Sayville and Aunt Beyrl's. Johnny asked no questions. He wanted no lies. He waved as the bus headed north.

Aunt Beyrl was a widow by then. Buster, the deceased stationery store owner, left Beyrl the business as part of a prenuptial agreement. The store ran itself, and Aunt Beyrl continued to sleep into the day. Not the girls.

Sayville and nearby Patchogue proved to be gold mines for their street band. They hustled Friday, Saturday, and Sunday. When the last Davis Park express ferry departed, the ladies' tip jar yielded at least a hundred bucks. For the remainder of the week, they lounged on Fire Island.

Having come of age on the Great South Bay, I understood the excitement Davis Park and Leja Beach generated. And yes, temptation's priorities, too. On an enticing moonlit evening the "Keep off the Sand Dunes" signs did little to discourage lovers and a blanket. As one might suspect, the Skipper twins were allured by the benefits of the casual beach lifestyle.

Thoughtful Dawn mailed Johnny a weekly postcard from the Davis Park Post Office.

This may sound screwy, but serendipity and synchronicity were about to create an exciting twist for Elmo French and the alluring Skipper sisters. The summer was about to heat up.

❋ ❋ ❋

One Friday evening, the last express water tax to Davis Park was delayed. The crowd grew impatient. "Why the delay?" asked Deidre. "Heavy traffic on the Southern State Parkway. We are waiting for some big shot from Manhattan," someone in the crowd complained.

Of course, the so-called "big shot" was Elmo French. Elmo spent a bachelor's holiday on Fire Island while Sylvia continued cohabitating with her guru in India. Elmo rented a two-story beach retreat on Bay Berry Walk overlooking the wetlands and the Great South Bay.

Elmo stepped from the limo and immediately spotted the twins. "Ladies, are you waiting for the water taxi to Davis Park?"

"No," Deidre replied.

"Well, I wish you were," Elmo said. "Do you live around here?" Elmo upped the game.

"No sir, my sister and I live in Fairden, South Carolina."

"Get out! No, you don't."

"Yes, we do," insisted Dawn.

"For goodness sake. I live in Fairden for the time being. Now isn't that a coincidence?"

You guessed it. Before you could say lickety-split, several deckhands were loading the Skippers and their band equipment onto a water taxi bound for Davis Park.

* * *

As Labor Day approached, it was time for the twins to say goodbye to Aunt Beyrl and take the bus to Fairden. The sisters squabbled over who would break the news to Johnny about their summer adventure with Elmo French.

"I'll do it," said Deidre."Might as well deal with it sooner rather than later."

Faithful Johnny was waiting at the bus terminal when the sisters arrived.

Dawn stepped off the bus, hugged Johnny, and said, "Dawn and I spent part of the summer on Fire Island with a millionaire."

Johnny was stunned. He pleaded to know why.

"He's wealthy, Johnny. The best things in life ain't free." Deidre was blunt and harsh.

"But he lacks your vigorous masculine spirit when you're not tired," Dawn reassured Johnny.

"He can't match you under the sheets. But Elmo French is filthy rich. So, we'll give him a pass," Deidre added.

"Johnny, we love you. But thanks to Elmo, we can kiss our street band days goodbye. No more groveling for tips on weekends. Elmo pays for everything. Oh, Johnny, I'll always love you." Dawn tried to dispel Johnny's fears.

"That goes for me, too," said Deidre. "You're our backup man if Elmo has extended downtime," Deidre added.

❊ ❊ ❊

Johnny's pride was hurt. Break a heart, and the pain lasts for a lifetime. Bruise a soul, and the pain lasts for eternity. Johnny grew angry. "Well, I'll show those two!" Johnny mumbled as he abandoned the twins at the bus terminal.

"Johnny come back," pleaded Dawn. "We need a ride home."

❊ ❊ ❊

Johnny was a man of action quick to respond but often with an irrecoverable flair.

When the ambulance arrived, the EMTs found a weeping, agonizing Johnny Scrubbs sitting on the Skipper's front stoop. A blood-splattered sheet draped Johnny's lap.

Florence, one of the EMTs, was Johnny's high school acquaintance. She slowly lifted the sheet and cringed in horror. She exclaimed, "Why did you do it, Johnny?"

"I wanted to punish the twins," he sobbed.

"Thank god the tip is only avulsed. It's hanging by a thread." Florence gently wrapped the extremity and rushed Johnny to the hospital. To a degree, the surgery was a success. Nevertheless, the story has a happy ending.

On a happy note, several years later, Johnny married Florence, and from all reports, they remain a loving couple.

❊ ❊ ❊

"Think of Johnny Scrubbs before you hastily act in anger. Cutting off you nose to spite your face only makes problems worse. It's also *a tender reminder* to look to the future and keep your best interests at heart."

Max Trotter

CHAPTER TWENTY-SEVEN

"I'm Not Good Enough."

Max finally worked up the courage to telephone the therapist that Matt recommend. Max wasn't about to go on antidepressants.

The following week, Max anxiously waited in Julie Myers' outer office. Max wiped droplets of perspiration from his forehead. I'm not going to get into the nitty-gritty, but here is the crux of Max's therapy session.

Ms. Myers appeared from behind the doorway of the inner office. First her head, then a shoulder, followed by her torso and finally by the entire five foot, three-inch frame. Ms. Myers looked very professional. She wore a conservative pantsuit, a blue woman's dress shirt that deterred prying eyes, and closed-toed flat shoes. Her blonde hair was tied in a bun just above her neck. A pair of horn rimmed glass were perched on her head.

"Max?"

"Yes." Max handed Ms. Myers several pages of forms attached to a clipboard.

"Please come into my office and have a seat."

"Is it okay to bring this cup of coffee?"

"You betcha and please call me Julie. Please sit down," Julie said. She spoke with a midwestern twang.

Max forced a smile and lowered himself into a couch that nearly swallowed him. Julie sat on the edge of what appeared to be a most uncomfortable desk chair. A yellow legal pad was within reach. Max kept glancing at the clock as though he was running out of time.

The two conversed about their backgrounds and professional careers. Max resisted any level of disclosure.

"Tell me Max, what brings you here today?"

Max avoided Julie's question.

At some point Max asked Julie, "Is this how therapy works? I make a statement and you pick up on it with an interrogative and attach my feelings to it?"

Max glanced at the clock. Time seemed to stand still.

"Is that your view of therapy, Max?"

"I don't know. Never been to a therapist before. We covered a lot of ground, but nothing specific," Max replied.

"It was the first question I asked," Julie responded. "When we spoke on the phone, you seemed to be going through a difficult time, recently. How are you feeling now?"

Max shrugged. "I don't know."

"As I recall, you told me this meeting was about your marriage, but you haven't mentioned your wife or your marriage. Is there something else you want to discuss?"

"My marriage, yes. My wife, Ann. And then there's my friend Elmo French. He is pressuring me to organize a band," Max said.

"Jeez, that's a lot," Julie remarked and smiled.

And then Max blurted, "Laura. Laura Finley. We were in a relationship. How did I let her get away? Yes, I want to talk about Laura."

"What do you mean you let her get away?"

"There you go again, Julie. You are turning my statement into a question."

Julie's eyes looked to the right and then the left. Then she leaned forward a bit and asked, "So, the relationship is over?"

"Yes. I think so. I'm not sure. Women confuse me. I called Laura a number of times. Laura finally returned my calls. She asked me to stop calling. She's met someone."

"And that was it?"

"No. Laura told me to go home to my wife. And then the phone went silent. I called back but she wouldn't answer. It wasn't my intention to stalk Laura, but one day I did drive to her condo. I couldn't get through the gate. Laura removed my name from her guest list.

"How did you feel when Laura told you to go back to Ann?"

"Confused. But there's more to it. It's like Laura has vanished. Like she never existed. The entire affair is like a bad dream, another mistake. How can I go home to Ann? I don't want to die in a loveless marriage. I have so much on my mind. Somedays my brain races faster than I can keep up with it."

"And you'd like to slow things down?"

"Yes."

" Max, you've been married for a long time. You and Ann have a lot of baggage. Some couples find themselves running in circles; the same arguments reoccur, but are never resolved."

"I've made a lot of mistakes."

Julie paused as though to underscore what she was about to say. "If you dwell on your mistakes, you will feel ashamed. Perhaps, you might discuss this with a friend."

"Julie, we live in a world of public shaming. Social media is swamped with stories of a friend betraying a confidence, the slightest indiscretion. It's difficult to trust anyone. Where did I go wrong?"

"Let's wait until our next session to deal with that question," said Julie. "Same time next week?" she asked.

"I'll check my calendar and call you, replied Max . He scratched his head and wondered what the last fifty minutes had accomplished.

* * *

Later that evening at Jugz.

Max pointed to a table in a far corner. He wanted to keep his conversation between the three of us. I was happy the Skipper sisters were bowling. I paid for three coffees and carried them to the table.

"So, how did it go with the shrink, Max?"

"Forget it, Elmo. It's confidential."

"We're your buddies, Max," Elmo insisted.

"Then you will understand."

"Laura's found someone else. Right?"

"Elmo, I don't want to get into it. You're prodding me to reveal a convoluted relationship. I respect Laura."

"Nonsense. You're holding out on us. Don't worry. Sooner or later, she'll get around to the sex."

"Who?" Max asked.

"Your therapist."

"Don't go there, Max. Julie Myers would never cross ethical boundaries."

I couln't help myself and said, "Max is right, Elmo. Friends encourage friends. I think you are messing with Max's head."

Just then the Skipper sisters arrived.

Dawn's "Hello" wave and her blue, laced romper caught everyone's attention.

Not to be outdone by Dawn, Deidre was semi-attired in a black plunging romper. She kissed Elmo, spun around, leaned over, and gave Max an asphyxiating hug.

Max blushed.

"Max don't blush. It's okay," said Deidre. "Every guy in the place would like a hug from me."

I wondered, but didn't ask, *No hug for me?*

"Max, how did your meeting with the shrink go?" Dawn shouted from the counter as she returned with two 8-ounce

Teasers.

"Damn it, Elmo. You told the Skippers."

"Max, I can't keep anything from these two. The girls and I have a wager going."

"About me?"

"The girls are betting you won't last more than two sessions with the shrink."

"Why?"

"Because you are too shy and too cautious," Deidre answered. Deidre enjoys a sarcastic barb.

"And what about you, Max?"

"Given that baby face and your needy vulnerability, your shrink will fall in love with you as fast as you can say 'libido.'"

"Then she can't be your shrink. So, I bet you're good for one more session," said Dawn.

Dawn and Deidre lost the bet. Max did return and for more than one session.

❋ ❋ ❋

The following week at Julie Myer's office.

"So, where was I?" Max asked.

"At our last session you told me about your band and your friend, Elmo French," Julie said.

Max nervously nodded. "And Laura, too."

"Of course."

"Max smiled and continued. "Talking about Elmo makes me anxious. Let's change the topic."

"It's your time, Max. Lead the way." Julie smiled.

"I told you I met Laura. But we are no longer dating."

Julie leaned a bit forward in her chair to accentuate her interest. "You are no longer dating?"

Max tilted his head to one side. *I'm convinced Julie uses*

psychological tricks. I'm not ready to reveal my inner most secrets.

"Tell me more." Julie coaxed him on.

"Where to begin?"

"As I recall from our last session, Laura told you to go home to you wife. That was interesting."

"It's complicated," Max replied. *Should I confess my conversation with Matt when I asked him to create Laura's character? No. Julie will think I am nuts.*

Max paused. "We were intimate, but only once."

"Intimate?"

Max rubbed his wrinkled forehead.

"Max you look perplexed."

"Well, kind of. We made love one evening at Laura's place. Of course, I'm guilt-ridden. I misled her. I should have told her I needed the pills."

Julie's eyes lit up. She clasped her hands in anticipation. "How did you mislead Laura, Max?"

Max bowed his head. "I told you it's complicated."

Julie turned to her desk and jotted something on the yellow legal pad.

"I feel uncomfortable when you turn toward your desk and write on that pad," Max said.

"Uncomfortable?"

"Yes, very. It's like you've discovered a major point about me. Some weakness or something? Mind telling me the comment you noted?"

"Of course I'll share it with you." Julie turned to pad and Max leaned over to read the note.

"Self-worth?" Max laughed. "And what does that mean?"

Julie paused and and segued. "At our last session you suggested it was too soon to start a relationship. You and Ann aren't divorced. What happened?"

"I don't know. I'm confused. Isn't that why I'm here?"

"You tell me, Max." Max's face turned blotchy. A minute or two passed in silence.

"I felt it was a good idea to avoid a serious relationship.

How did I know that Laura would walk into my life?" Max shifted on the couch. He gazed out the window.

Julie sensed Max's thoughts were drifting. "Are you okay?"

"Yes, but something just doesn't feel right."

"How so?" Julie asked.

"It's exhausting living a life of postponed dreams, while at the same time attempting to do the right thing. You know. What others expect."

Julie asked, "Do you mean 'mind reading?'"

"That's it exactly. Trying to mind read."

"Anticipating and pleasing others while all the time knowing you are setting yourself up for failure?" Julie asked.

"Yes. Exactly. And that's when I feel like, a failure." Max took a deep breath and exhaled. "Men and women are so different," he said.

"Yes, they can be," Julie agreed. "I find men are more reluctant to share their deep concerns and fears, but when they do they often find compassion. Women are more open to discuss their intimacies. Nevertheless, the seem to feel they receive less compassion."

"That's not Laura. She's frank about her needs. Max's face reddened. "She's not embarrassed. That's why I admire her." Max paused. "Laura hasn't returned a single call. I'm afraid I've lost her. She had terrific insight. I'm sure Laura suspected I wasn't over Ann."

"Max, do you have a trusted friend?"

"I'm not sure anymore. I tried talking with Elmo French. He laughs and tells me my troubles are all in my head."

"Perhaps another person you trust. It helps to have a friend who is a good listener." Julie glanced at the wall clock. "Our time is about up, Max."

"Please give me a moment," he insisted. "After our last meeting, I wondered if a day will come when I'm able to recall the happy moments from my marriage."

Julie looked puzzled.

"Life is lived in the 'now,' Max. Enjoy it," Julie replied. "Shall we schedule another appointment?"

Max pushed himself of the couch. "No. I'll call. Please give me some time. Therapy is a lot tougher than I thought it would be."

Max surveyed Julie's quiet grace as she escorted him to the private exit. But it was her intellect the captured his imagination.

❄ ❄ ❄

"Happiness is letting go of what you think your life is supposed to look like. It also helps to have a poor memory."
Unkown

CHAPTER TWENTY-EIGHT

"At The End Of The Day"

Max stopped at Jugz the other evening. He found Elmo and me engrossed in conversation, minus the Double D's.

"Elmo, where are the twins?" Max asked.

"They flew to Manhattan to purchase lingerie."

"Couldn't they purchase underwear on the Internet?"

"Yes. Nonetheless, 'Pleasurements' is an erotica fashion brand, and the twins love in-store purchases."

"I'm a man of simple tastes and enjoy flannel," Max insisted.

"You and Matt, live in a shoe. As for me, the twins delight in fulfilling my fantasies."

I shrugged. *A few days ago, Elmo complained that the Double D's are extravagant and max-out his credit card.*

The conversation became revealing.

Max said, "I dated a fabulous woman. She was bold and flirtatious. I was a simple country boy. Admittedly, it took months before I mastered the one-handed bra stap move."

Elmo smirked. "You, two, are a couple of old geeks."

"Elmo, speak for yourself," I admonished.

Max continued. "When Ann and I dated, she was a moody, seductive, adventurous fox. She is still beautiful but reserved, feminine, and sophisticated."

"What happened?" I asked.

Max paused, stirred his 12-ounce Sassy and looked directly at me. "We got married."

❋ ❋ ❋

We continued to talk, but Max started paging through a book. Surprisingly, Max paid little attention to Elmo's panty preferences. We turned to Max.

"Max, why are you reading *Where The Wild Things Are?* It's a children's book. Where's your iPad? Jugz caters to adults."

" People are staring at you," said Elmo.

"Exactly, Elmo." Max looked at us with determination and said, "The story's hero is named Max. That's my name, too. Except, I'm no hero. And you know what? These days there are fearsome monsters out there. But story book Max, our hero, knows ,'If you stare into all their yellow eyes without blinking once, you can tame them and temper them and get home before supper gets cold.'"

"*Where the Wild Things Are i*s one of my favorite children's stories," I said. "Emma's Bookstore sells lots of copies."

"Don't say that too loudly. *Where the Wild Things Are* is on the banned book list because it causes anxiety in adults," said Elmo.

"Matt, perhaps one day, if I am lucky, my faux memoir will be banned, too. Then folks are sure to purchase it."

Max yawned. It was getting close to his bedtime. He finished his coffee and said, "Good night."

"Hold on, Max," ordered Elmo. "When are you going to put together a garage band?"

Max shrugged and said, "In time."

Now here's the dig. Elmo huffed. "Sure, just like your missing girlfriend, Laura Finley, a garage band is only a dream."

❋ ❋ ❋

"How do you know I am mad?" said Alice.

"You must be," said the Cat, or you wouldn't have come here."

Lewis Carroll

CHAPTER TWENTY-NINE

"Puppy Love"

Greetings. It's me again, Matt Nagle. Elmo was always prodding Max, not as though he was grooming a new recording celebrity, but rather like chipping paint from the side of a timeworn house. The two had many hilarious conversations, but this one was serious. One day, Max was feeling angst.

"I read that the act of dream sharing increases empathy. I had an unsettling dream and want to share it with both of you."

"So, what's bothering you, my friend?" asked Elmo.

"My dream was about a girl I dated in high school."

"Knowing you, Max, that's when you fell in love for the first time, right?"

"No, that's not it, Matt."

"I'll bet. Seems you are preoccupied with your love life," replied Elmo.

Like most men, Max was afraid to reveal his vulnerability, even to Elmo, a trusted friend. But tonight, Max decided to confide in Elmo.

Unfortunately, Elmo had become a card-carrying romantic cynic since Sylvia abandoned him.

"Damn it, Elmo. I patiently listen to you, but you blow me off when I tell you something that's worrying me."

"But Max, you are always so serious."

"Elmo, you place people into emotionless boxes and allow them out when it suits." Max pushed against the table, spilling his coffee.

"Hey. Where are you going?"

"What do you care?" Max muttered.

"You left a mess," Elmo barked.

"You're right. Clean it up!"

Elmo shrugged and mumbled, "Okay", and wiped the spilled coffee onto the floor, and thought no more about the incident. That's just the way Elmo dealt with things.

Elmo's indifference upset Max. Still, he couldn't shake off the urge to tell someone about a particular time in his life. But who could he trust? He turned to me, Matt Nagle. By now, you know that Max often speaks introspectively and deeply. So, I hope he doesn't object to me sharing a few insights, with you.

❈ ❈ ❈

A few days later, Max turned to me. "Matt, I need a friend."

"Of course Max, I can tell there is something urgent you need to get off your chest."

Max smiled. "Would you like a coffee, first?"

"Not just yet, Max." I sensed Max felt nervous revealing a coming-of-age tale about living on the second floor of Uncle John's funeral home.

"Were you lonely?" I asked Max.

"Not really. Serenity Funeral Home was one of the most traditional-looking homes in Patchogue. Everyone called it "Uncle John's." Uncle John took pride in the vast front porch with rocking chairs and plenty of ashtrays. To this day, I love porches. They are a wonderful place to sit back and rummage through misplaced memories.

❈ ❈ ❈

Max described the ornate viewing chapel. "It could be

divided into two even smaller rooms just in case Uncle John had a busy week. Now and then, I'd meander downstairs unnoticed. Most folks appeared preoccupied with their grief. And the others were too busy talking."

"People don't stick around funeral homes for long. They view the deceased, pay respects to family members, and get the hell out of there."

"Max, what about your friends?" I asked.

"I had a few. But winters up north are cold. I didn't play outside. And friends couldn't come in. When I turned ten, Uncle John put me to work in the mortuary. That kept me busy after school."

Max recalled his schoolmates and bullies calling him and his family weird.

"I didn't understand their perspective until I was in high school. I turned eighteen my senior year of high school."

I listened attentively to Max's tale, but I kept recalling my own childhood. I felt an impulse to say, "Max give yourself a break. There's dysfunctionality in all families." But for some reason I didn't

Oddly enough, the thought of a funeral home lifestyle sounded a bit incongruous to me, but who was I to reflect on life inside Serenity? Besides, these are Max's memories, not mine.

* * *

It was getting late. I needed to return to Emma's Bookstore before closing. I was about to excuse myself when Max held out his hand and said, "Matt thanks for being a good friend and a good listener." We shook hands.

Max's expression grew serious. "Thanks for listening, Matt. "Sometime in the future I would love to share a pivotal moment in my life. Her name was Kate. And I was a teenager with uncharted emotions."

CHAPTER THIRTY

"Kate"

Kate Murphy was a popular senior. Max was shy and preferred the library to the athletic field. Max glanced at Kate each morning on his way to history class or was it chemistry? It doesn't matter. The critical thing is Max gathered enough courage to ask her on a date.

Max never could figure out why she agreed. "I'll call you this evening," he said. Max was so anxious that he forgot to ask for Kate's telephone number.

It didn't take long for Max to have an "aha" moment. Max had never been on a date. That sudden realization plunged him into a quandary. He hadn't thought the whole thing out. Max rarely acted spontaneously.

"PPC" – Probabilities. Preplanning. Contingencies. Uncle John preached "PPC" each night at supper. "When you're in my profession, you never know when the phone will ring."

"Living in The Serenity Funeral Home, I learned that life changes in an instant." Max said. He frowned.

"No room for impulsiveness. Serenity's regime probably explained why Max's father, Burt, wore the customary funeral home uniform - black suit, white shirt, tie, and polished black shoes - from sunrise to sunset. He always wore an apron when he polished the hearse and the two limousines. Burt was always on call for a home pickup."

How in the world was Max going to take Kate on a date?

* * *

Max had a driver's license, but he didn't own a car. Uncle John let Max drive the hearse for his road test.

"For sure, I wasn't going to ask my father to chauffeur us to the movies. That would create an embarrassing high school humiliation," Max told me.

As luck would have it, Burt placed a down payment on a new Cadillac.

"Buy whatever," replied Uncle John at learning the news. "Remember, it must be a black Cadillac Fleetwood sedan," Uncle John insisted.

Erica, Max's resolute mother, demanded the shoal green edition.

"It just wouldn't look right," replied Uncle John. "What will people think? Tradition calls for black cars. I can't have a shoal green sedan in my driveway."

"My dad, was always intimidated by my Uncle John and my mother. Dad impetuously canceled the car order without consulting my mother, a grave sin."

That evening, after supper, Max mustered enough courage to tell his father two things.

"Dad, I've asked a girl on a date for Friday night." Then he mumbled, "I really need permission to use one of the cars."

Burt stifled a laugh. "You mean one of Uncle John's limousines? Where are you planning to take the young lady?"

"Just to the movies, to the diner, and home."

"I better ask your mother first before I ask Uncle John for his okay," Burt responded, avoiding eye contact. "In any case, I want you home by ten o'clock."

"Dad, the girl doesn't have to be home until eleven."

"We'll discuss the particulars later. A real date, Max? I'm astonished."

Max knew his father wanted to say "yes," but Burt always consulted with Erica before agreeing to anything. Erica Trotter ran a tight ship. Right from the giddyup, Erica held the nuptial reins. She left the big decisions to Burt - like when to launch a thermonuclear war. And on this particular evening Erica was feeling ornery and short on forgiveness after Burt canceled the shoal green Caddy.

So, Burt faced a dilema when Erica gave a "thumbs-down." Erica wanted no part of indebtedness to Uncle John.

The following day, a defiant Burt, hat in hand, worked up enough courage to approach his brother.

As for Uncle John it was two words,"No way."

"I'll have to tell Erica," said Burt.

Social psychologists have identified 125 biases, not all inappropriate. Uncle John had his own biases including mice in the mortuary. But the topper was his sister-in-law, Erica, whom Uncle John shunned and feared.

"Hold on. I have an idea," said Uncle John. "The 1950 Cadillac hearse that the fire department used as an ambulance. It's been sitting in the back yard for a while. Still has license plates. That's it! Take it or leave it," Uncle John declared.

Burt looked puzzled. "John, can you imagine the ridicule Max will face when he pulls up to the girl's home driving a hearse?"

"It was proudly sponsored by my funeral home. Remove the signage from the doors."

Knowing his brother would not give in, Burt reluctantly agreed. He'd take the ambulance.

That evening a sad-faced Max carelessly twirled his spaghetti and pouted. "Dad, I'll be the laughing stock."

"I'll give you money for a cab, or I'll drive you, myself," Burt responded.

"And so Matt, put yourself in my place. What choice did I have?"

I shrugged. "I guess you took the ambulance."

❄ ❄ ❄

Max and his dad went to work just after sunrise the following morning. Burt wore a white apron over his black suit, white shirt and tie. He poured a couple of bottles of his cure-all, Pepsi, through the carburetor. He changed the oil. Thanks to his apron, Burt completed the tune-up without getting a drop of oil or grease on his white shirt or tie. A trifle mysterious, I agree.

Max scrubbed the interior and vacuumed the floor. He stood back to admire the work. *It hardly makes a difference.*

Nevertheless, when Friday night arrived, Max gave his dad a big hug. "Thanks dad." Then in a cloud of dark exhaust smoke, Max proudly drove the revived ambulance, the siren still worked, around the circular driveway and headed east.

Burt waved his undertaker's tophat and shouted "Max, remember to check the brake fluid from time to time."

✻ ✻ ✻

An anxious Max spotted Kate's house. Max could hear his stomach rumbling its chronic response. He glanced in the rear-view mirror. He combed his hair one more time, and frowned at his complexion.

Parking the hearse was another challenge. *Mission accomplished.*

Max climbed the porch steps. A stern-looking woman opened the front door.

"Hello. I'm Max," he mumbled as he reached the front door. Max always mumbled when he was nervous.

The woman scowled as she moved from the front door into the kitchen. The huge kitchen table was the center of family activity.

"My name is Andrea. Come in and sit down," she ordered. Andrea turned out to be Kate's much older sister. Max learned that no one called her "Andi." *A nickname didn't fit her personality.*

Max forced a smile and squirmed attempting to look past Andrea. *No sign of Kate. What was keeping her? Maybe Kate changed her mind.*

"Where are you taking Kate?" Andrea asked.

"To a movie."

Andrea sensed Max was nervous and exploited the opportunity to amuse herself with a bit of big sister harassment.

Suddenly, the door burst open and in bounded a boy Max recognized from school. It turned out to be Andrea's son. He opened the refrigerator door then turned and asked, "Hey man want a Seven-Up?"

"Yes, thanks." Max fumbled with the bottle opener. Andrea seized the bottle and popped the cap.

"Here!" she huffed. "Don't spill it."

"So let me ask you again. Where are you two headed tonight? My parents want to know," Andrea demanded.

"The movies, I think. At least that's what we talked about in school," Max apprehensively responded.

"No football? There is an away game at East Islip. And you aren't going?"

"My dad won't let me drive that far." Andrea and the boys broke out laughing.

Max panicked. *Why did I say that?*

Max quickly tried to shift gears. "I usually work Friday and Saturday nights until eight. I switched my hours."

Then, the tempo suddenly changed. "Well, I must get back to work. Kate will be out in a minute."

"Ah, Max, don't worry. Kate keeps all the boys waiting. A piece of advice. Stay away from the marina. Our father disapproves."

Just as Max decided enough was enough, Kate appeared. She looked even more beautiful than she did in school. "Okay. I'm ready if you are," Kate said. "Let's get going."

❋ ❋ ❋

"I don't recall the movie, maybe the 'Magnificent Seven.' I do remember going to the diner that evening. Our classmates, practically all Kate's friends, began drifting in. The girls and maybe one or two boys came to our table and talked with Kate. One guy gave me a skeptical look, like 'What's Kate doing with this doofus?'"

"I drove Kate home."

"Don't walk me to the door. I know you need to get home," Kate said.

"I raced home. It was nearly eleven o'clock when I parked the Beast, my name for the old Cadillac, which would play an essential part in my coming of age. I'm sure mom and dad were asleep."

The following day dad asked, "Did you have a nice time last night, Max?"

"Yes, sir. It was a wonderful evening."

My parents smiled at one another, but nothing more was said.

❋ ❋ ❋

I don't know what possessed Uncle John, but to my amazement, he allowed me to drive the Beast to school. At lunch time, a bunch of Kate's friends gathered in the parking lot. I was geared-up for some mean-spirited taunts. On the contrary, most of the guys thought the hearse was cool.

"Max, you've got some balls driving a hearse for your personal car."

I turned around to find Bobby Sugar pretending to polish

the Beast with the sleeve of his varsity jacket.

"Max, I'm putting a band together. I heard you play."

Bobby had a reputation of bona fide ladies' man, and outstanding guitarist. I could understand. He wore his long black hair slicked backed with Brylcreem. The heavy scent of Aqua Velva Ice Blue added to Bobby's charisma.

"Bobby, I'm no rocker," I stammered.

"That's what I figured. You'll learn. And ditch those penny loafers. So do you want to join my band? We need your hearse, too. We've got heavy amps and speakers."

"Sure thing." I knew Bobby wanted the hearse.

❃ ❃ ❃

It's time for the Beast.

The Beast was big, slow, and ugly. Yet, for Max, their love affair was a gift from heaven. Max promised, no vowed, to care for her. In turn, the Beast promised freedom. Max and the Caddy hearse went steady for the next five years filled with drive-in movies, submarine race watching and beach parties.

Sadly, the Beast's transmission failed. Max was short on cash. The Beast's repairs cost more than a run-down 1959 VW. Max needed wheels.

Max stored the Beast behind the funeral home. One day, Max's now-deceased Uncle John, God bless his grumpy soul, gave Max's beauty to a cousin who fixed her up enough to go one round in a Demolition Derby.

"Oh Beast, forgive me," Max sighed.

❃ ❃ ❃

I sipped my coffee and intently listened to Max's story.

"So Max, to change the subject, tell me more about

submarine race watching."

"As I recall, it was all very innocent. Kids parked in some secluded spot and made-out. If we parked by the water we'd say the couple parked to watch the submarine races. The marina will always be special for me. I love the Great South Bay."

"Yes. You make it sound like a magical place, Max."

"It is special, Matt. But only those who parked there to watch the sunset on a warm summer evening will ever know."

"So what happened to Kate Murphy?"

✳ ✳ ✳

"Like most high school romances, things fell apart. It was totally my fault. But this isn't the time to get into it." Max's eyes momentarily closed as though he was drifting to another place in time.

"That's it?" I asked.

"I remember one night in May sitting alone on the marina dock listening to Cousin Bruce. He played Roy Orbinson's, "Only The Lonely.""

Max scowled. "For a while, I wandered in and out of unhappiness, feeling unlovable."

"I know that feeling. I thought I had a monopoly on emptiness," I remarked.

"Like I said, I was to blame. Inevitably, I created my own reality. I never liked being vulnerable. No tears. No recriminations." Max's eyes turned toward the floor.

"That's scary coming from you, Max. But you don't have to punish yourself. You were a teenager; a lonely one at that."

"I agree, Matt. It was creepy. Matt, you are an exceptional listener."

I forced a smile. Still, Max was acting mighty peculiar. He has frequent moments of melancholy.

"I love the Great South Bay. There! I've said it again," Max confessed.

"Max, earlier you told me about your first kiss. Was that when you fell in love for the first time?"

"Between the two of us, Matt, I fell in love a number of times. Each time it began with a kiss. And now, after all these years, my high school and college memories seem like musical interludes - the saxophone instrumentals and Doo Wop passages that come between the lyrics of 'In the Still of the Night.' Did they ever exist?"

Max's comment fascinated me. I've come to the conclusion that there is a danger for older men to revisit their youth and those magic moments.

* * *

"Max, your insights never fail to amaze me."

"Matt, I discovered my memory is fickle like my wardrobe. I mix and match without giving much regard to the colors or for that matter, the seasons. Nonetheless, thinking back there is one, perhaps frivolous constant, my penny loafers. I've been wearing cordovan penny loafers since high school. I don't remember the shoes I wore when performing with Bobby Sugar, but I know I didn't wear penny loafers. I can't explain it, but each time I slip into my penny loafers, I get a warm comfortable feeling."

Perhaps, Max's recollections of falling in love were a romanticized potpourri of adolescent infatuations. Later that evening I began searching through Max's notes for a clue.

* * *

It was nearly midnight as I browsed Max's notebooks. I discovered a page with several sentences. I recognized Max's messy handwriting.

"She kissed me" was scribbled across the top of one page. I don't know what possessed me, but I called Max.

"Matt, do you know what time it is?"

"Sorry Max, but I had to call. I read the brief entry to Max. "Do you want me to include the note in your memoir?"

There was a long pause.

"Matt that was a defining moment in my life. We were listening to Murray The K on the radio. I told you, it was nothing more than a kiss."

"Max, that's so romantic coming from you. I always pictured you as a cynic. But that one unfinished sentence remains. And who gave you the kiss?"

"Let's leave it that way, Matt. I'm an old man. Listening to you read my note reassures me that those happy times were a real and filled with anticipation."

I didn't reply.

"Again, please don't include the note in my memoir. And Matt, let's not discuss it again."

Max is right. Sometimes it's the simple things in life that leave the lasting impression.

❋ ❋ ❋

"There is a danger for older men to revisit their youth. The hase of memory raises an uncertainty of the mind and overshadows an enduring truth."
Max Trotter

CHAPTER THIRTY-ONE

"Slices"

Here are a few more slices I gleaned from Max's notes. They reveal Max's sensitive and romantic side.

Each evening after work, Max drove to Tony's Italian Restaurant and parked the Beast near the LIRR Station. He was amazed watching inebriated passengers stumble off the eastbound Bar Car. A number of them walked across the tracks to Tony's.

"Matt, I know now that hanging out at Tony's -accepting drinks, screwdrivers, from lonely older women was no place for a high school senior."

Nevertheless, I believed Max when he said, "I felt comfortable among Tony's cast of characters."

At first, Tony's wasn't as dear to Max as the reference room in the Patchogue Library, where he pretended to be studying while meticulously staying within the lines of a Looney Tunes coloring book. But, as winter turned into spring, the library became stale. The library lacked the aroma of hot pizza, the ambiance of an easy-listening jazz pianist, and a glimpse of cheaters at a dimly lit corner table.

And like many of Tony's regulars, Max didn't want to leave. Still, after the pizza and screwdrivers, Max headed home. His homework awaited.

❋ ❋ ❋

The day came when young Max needed to unburden the

real pain of his teenage breakup.

Max trusted his teacher, Mr. Thomas. Max sensed Mr. Thomas was well-practiced at keeping secrets. Mr. Thomas was a good listener. "I feel you're hurting, Max. What's going on?"

There isn't much time in between high school classes, but Mr. Thomas didn't need much time.

Mr. Thomas placed his hand on Max's shoulder - a gesture that in today's world might cost Mr. Thomas his job - and said, "I lost the person I loved. Not quite like what you're going through, but in some ways the same."

"Yes, you were mean-spirited to break that girl's heart without an explanation, Max," Mr. Thomas agreed. "Look at me, Max. You may fall in and out of love a million times. Give yourself some time."

Max was astonished. He'd never heard Mr. Thomas call a student by his first name.

Then, without offering additional advice, Mr. Thomas said, "Get to class Trotter. I don't write late passes."

❋ ❋ ❋

"You can fix almost anything but a borken heart"
Guy Winch

❋ ❋ ❋

"Matt, one of my favorite books is *Big Fish*. The main character, Edward Bloom, confides, 'They say when you meet the love of your life, time stops, and that's true.'"

"All in all, my high school years had their ups and downs, too," I told Max. "But time does stop when you fall in love. That's what happened when I met Liz in college," I said.

Max continued. "Ann and I never reminisced about our romance before we married. Now, mentioning our roller coaster marriage ranks number one on Ann's 'no-no' list of the top five socially incorrect cocktail party topics.

"What are the other four?," I asked.

2. Complaining about the night before my colonoscopy.

3. Preserving dead mice.

4. Revealing I was raised in a funeral home.

5. Presumed "gay".

"Come to think of it Max, considering the Covid vaccination controversies, some folks might feel uncomfortable discussing funeral homes over cheese and crackers. But what's this about "presumed gay?" I asked.

"You know how folks are at our age. The confusing male stereotype of course. It's embedded in men over sixty. Women too," Max added.

"From my perspective Max, women like a touch of femininity in their male partners."

"Agreed. Still, other women step back and reject a man with those traits," Max replied.

"I don't see the problem Max. You know who you are. Where did you get that idea?"

"When I was in high school, Uncle John cautioned me to avoid doing anything that someone might consider feminine. 'Cut you own toe nails.' He never mentioned 'gay.' I came of age during the fifties. Along came the late sixties and seventies and all hell broke out. Woman seemed to go for the simpering vulnerable male. I loathe the whole damn conundrum."

Max slapped the side of his head as though to empty the remains of a Ketchup bottle, an unusual quirk that made him conspicuous on social occasions.

"God help us, Max. Today, it's open season on the LGBT community and the vulnerable. They are family members

– sons and daughters, nieces and nephews, our friends. Politician across our nation are turning our loved ones into political fodder by creating a climate of fear and hatred."

Max quickly looked over his shoulder as though someone might be listening to their conversation. "Matt, these are dangerous times to be truthful or to express feelings on scary topics that upset adults. You'll be labeled 'woke,' if you keep it up."

I tried to reassure Max that I understood where he was coming from. "Max, I'm beginning to agree with you. Nobody is honest when it come to the real personal stuff."

"Mat, I recall attending a Halloween block party. There were fifty people in attendance. I decided to dress like a French maid. It was all in fun.

A guy didn't realize I was a man. He asked me to dance. The next thing I knew, he touched my package. You should have seen the look on his face. He broke out in a cold sweat. It was hilarious."

It's not so funny today Max considering how gender issues have become a battle cry in the class conscious culture wars.

* * *

A few days later, Max called. "Matt, it's best if you scour my memoir slices and delete my remarks about presumed gay, or gender identity. I've decided that honesty and political correctness are double-edged swords. The politically correct handbook is expanding too quickly and these are dangerous times. I don't want to be the target of a "woke attack."

"Hold on Max. Which side may attack you?" I asked.

Max replied, "Both!"

* * *

"Knowing ourselves is a lifelong, bold and intimidating process. We fear this process because it lays us bare to criticism and rejection."

Dr. T.J. Jordon

CHAPTER THIRTY-TWO

"The Jam Session"

Max contemplated the move for months. What should I take? What to leave behind? He didn't take much; his passport, and whatever clothes he could pack into two suitcases.

Max blamed himself. After all, he was sneaking out of his home. He lacked the courage to leave while Ann was home. He briefly grappled with the thought of what his friends would think of him for abandoning his wife. But the idea vanished as he tossed the suitcases into his car.

Max took one last look around. He placed the note against the telephone.

Leaving is painful, but I can't make Ann love me if she won't.

❋ ❋ ❋

Max rarely invited anyone to his Great River condo. It was meagerly furnished. Perhaps just as well since two keyboards, speakers, and the rest of his electronics occupied most of the space. Cables from the mixing board ran along the floor across the living room and into the bedroom, where a microphone, earphones, and a music stand awaited the next vocal session. The bedspread served double duty as soundproofing for the far wall. Max placed the speakers in the far corners of the room and dampened them with blankets.

It took time to set up his electronics. So Max left

everything in place. Nevertheless, Max was organized, though not apparent to the casual eye. Get the picture? The arrangement was okay for a small jam session with one or two guys, maybe three.

Thanks to a few basic computer programs, Max had LA's hottest session players, Nashville hired guns, or New York's finest studio cats backing him up, all at the touch of a button and the voicing of a chord.

The exhausting work involved in the setup amplified Max's decision not to start a garage band.

"Keep it simple. Bring your ax and maybe a music stand and plug in," Max told the boys.

"Why only male musicians?" asked Elmo. "Dawn grooves on the sax and Diedre's bass guitar sounds tough and funky."

"Elmo, I'm not opposed to having a woman join our sessions, but not the Skipper sisters. Their flirting is bound to spell trouble."

❊ ❊ ❊

The music world had changed since Max played in Bobby Sugar's band. One thing had not changed. Sugar warned Max that bands pack it in for many reasons: money, the lack of commitment, frivolous disagreements, jealousy, bickering, drugs, and alcohol.

Max contemplated another downer, Elmo. Toss Elmo into the mix and disaster lurks in the background.

Elmo demanded Dawn and Deidre join the session.

Max folded his arms and stood his ground. "That doesn't work for me."

❊ ❊ ❊

It was two in the morning when Max reluctantly answered his phone.

"Max, what the hell are you doing?"

"Elmo, what's wrong?"

"You started a garage band without me?"

"No. We are just jamming."

"And you didn't invite the twins to sit in?"

"My apartment is small. The superintendent warned me about deafening music."

"Max the girls insist on being in your garage band."

"There's no band, Elmo."

"There will be. I'll scout studios for rehearsal time."

"Elmo, please. Let's talk about this in the morning," Max pleaded.

Like the Bible's persistent widow, Elmo was relentless. In the end Max folded.

❁ ❁ ❁

"If pleasing someone else comes at the cost of your own happiness and well-being, it isn't worth it."
Erin Eatough, PhD

CHAPTER THIRTY-THREE

"Where Are The Twins?"

I dropped by Jugz that afternoon for a bit of eavesdropping and a cup of coffee. It never fails. In walked Max and Elmo. Seems like everywhere I go, they turn up.

"Hey Matt, odd meeting you here," said Elmo.

"Hello Elmo. Where are the twins?"

"Down the street getting pedicures at the salon."

"That's your former establishment, Elmo. Do they get a discount?"

"To my chagrin, no discounts, Matt."

"Elmo, you pamper those two," I told him.

"I know," Elmo agreed. They demand a lot of attention."

"Speaking of discounts, Elmo. You own Jugz, but never offer us a complimentary mug of java," I remarked.

"I'm going broke. Do you have a problem balancing your check book Matt?"

Before I could respond, Elmo said, "Get this. My insurance provides me with six Viagra pills a month. I must pay full price for the other fifteen or twenty."

"Why not try the generic? Try cutting back on the sex. Consider your health rather than pampering two twenty-four-year-olds. Forget the Double D's for a moment and listen to me," I insisted.

"I can't forget them, Matt. They have my credit card. Do you have any idea of the cost of implants?"

"Elmo how can you afford those two precocious women? I predict an impending crisis in your future."

Elmo's face turned red as he began to reveal his predicament.

To this point Max was surprisingly quiet. Then he innocently exclaimed, "Sylvia told me you have a heart condition. I'm concerned. Since Sylvia left, you've fostered an unhealthy dependency on Dawn and Deidre. Granted they are a voluptuous, sensual, and indulgent pair."

Elmo laughed.

"Elmo, the Skipper sisters are masters of manipulation," Max insisted.

Elmo shot Max a quizzical expression.

"They are leading you around like a puppy on a leash. They compliment you and call you Daddy," I added.

"I like the attention, Matt. Sylvia never compliments me. I thought of her needs first, especially in bed." Elmo sounded increasingly insistent.

"If Sylvia really loved you, she wouldn't be galivanting around the posh Jor Bagh district of Delhi. And you are still sending her checks," Max said.

"I don't want Sylvia to return now that the Double D's have moved in. I called her paramour, Veer Shevade and warned him: 'Don't cheat on my wife.' I want her to remain with you in India."

"As for the Skippers, Dawn and Deidre lavish me with compliments. Sylvia always recalls my mistakes, like marrying the au pair."

"They use sex to manipulate you," said Max.

"It's their wardrobe that bothers you. Right? I urge them to wear more clothes."

"On the other hand, Dawn looks great in those shorts and alluring camisole tank top," Max confessed.

Max and Matt looked at one another. "Elmo, we could hit you over the head with a hammer and you still wouldn't acknowledge our point," I insisted.

"And what's that?"

"You enjoy being manipulated," said Max.

Elmo looked sullen. "Yes, but so what?" With that Elmo loosened his ascot and placed his bad-ass sunglasses on the table. "I don't give a damn what people think of the Skipper twins. The sexual tension energizes me. It's exhausting worrying about what others think of me. Did it ever occur to you that I might be using the twins rather than visa versa?"

"Hmm. I see your point," Max agreed.

"As far as my marriage goes, things are probably as good as they get," Elmo conceded. "By the way Max, I heard that you and Laura are no longer an item."

"Elmo, I'm not discussing the intimacies of my love life. But it is true."

"My question is where do the broken hearted go to ease the pain?" Max asked.

"Disney World." I responded. "Where else, but among the plastic people will you find somebody to love?"

"Wrong. Disney is woke. Haven't you heard? The best place go to is Jugz. Drown your sorrows in a 16-ounce Naughty mug of java," Elmo replied. "Misery deserves company. A lot of miserable people at Jugz these days."

"And Disney, too," Max replied.

"You should be enjoying your newly found freedom, Max. Maybe Elmo is on to something, Max," I said.

Suddenly, there was a clamor of excitement at the front entrance. Two guys were arguing about holding the door open for the voluptuous Double D's.

"Holy smokes, Elmo." I felt my eyes bug-out. The girls are scantily dressed, again," I remarked "If it wasn't for the jewelry they could be arrested for indecent exposure. You warned the ladies about causing a stir. This is a modest community."

"Calm down, men. I'm surprised by your remark, Matt. It's sexism plain and simple. You'll have a stroke. Nothing indecent about those two," Elmo replied. "They are just too demanding." Elmo rubbed his chest as though he was experiencing palpitations.

"Daddy, do you want the usual?" Deidre asked.

Elmo winked and nodded. The pair scampered to the counter.

I watched the twins at work. I pity Elmo. He refuses to see that the sisters are after his car, credit card, and home. Then again, I may be too harsh.

"Max, what's going on? I hardly see you anymore," said Dawn.

"Oh, I've had a couple of setbacks. It's not easy being a bachelor."

"Time will tell, Max," Dawn said.

I said, "Rarely does time reveal anything but age."

"I agree. I'm tired of walking into a fast food place and having the Senior Breakfast handed to me. I didn't want the damn thing. Do I look decrepit?" Max asked.

"That can be hurtful," Dawn agreed.

"There's a difference between getting old and aging," said Elmo.

Deidre laughed and shouted from the counter"Elmo is getting forgetful. He is always misplacing something. Usually in bed. Dawn is right, Daddy. There's a difference between forgetting where you tossed your car keys and not knowing what the keys are for."

The others laughed. Max shouted, "Brovo!"

"You guys are nuts," I said with a smile.

Deidre tiptoed to the table carrying Elmo's mocha latte like it was a glass of nitroglycerin. She sensually brushed Elmo's hand to one side, placed the cup on the table, and pulled her chair close to "Daddy." Dawn sneered. She appeared a bit jealous.

Elmo added, "I love the girls calling me 'Daddy.'"

"You're wicked, Elmo," I said. My comment didn't appear to trouble Elmo.

"Move over fatty," said Dawn to Deidre.

I surveyed Deidre's sleek torso. *If there is any fat on Deidre, I can't see it.*

Deidre caught my glance and winked.

* * *

"While we are on the topic of aging, tell Matt about your nursing home research, Daddy," said Deidre.

Matt looked askance.

"My assisted living insurance premium doubled this year."

"Please, not another nursing home orgy story."

"Give Elmo a chance," said Deidre.

"The twins patronize a top-dollar pleasure boutique," said Elmo.

"You want the best for us, Daddy," said Dawn.

"You tell the story, Deidre."

"Dawn and I were at the shop and helped an eighty-year-old blind woman struggling to purchase a sex toy. The nursing home bus stops at Dollar General, Walmart, and McDonald's for lunch."

Dawn interrupted. "The mean, sexually repressive, power-hungry bus driver refused to stop at Bawdy Lady. The old girl told me she paid for an Uber."

"Ladies you are exaggerating," Max insisted with a laugh.

"It's true, Max," Elmo insisted. Not only that, but the incident got me to increase my long term insurance benefits. I now have 'Plus Coverage.'"

"Plus, what?" asked Max.

"First, I added Uber to my coverage. And second, it's common knowledge that nursing home sexual activity invites problems including the increased risk of sexually transmitted diseases. It's expensive, but I added STD screening to be on the safe side."

"Good thinking, Daddy" asserted Deidre.

"Everyone deserves pleasure, Max," Dawn added. "Even if a guy is old, wrinkled, short and paunchy, he's still entitled to love."

"Not in today's world," said Elmo. "It's all about the money and technology. I've got the money, but beyond the little blue pill, I'm searching for a technological miracle."

"Oh Daddy. You worry too much. You have us," Deidre added.

❊ ❊ ❊

Then out of nowhere, Elmo brought up my book sales.

"Matt, I heard book sales aren't going well. Good thing you have the bookstore income. I'm always willing to help market your books."

"Sales are down. I'm tough skinned."

"A college friend called last evening. After some small talk he asked, 'How are your books selling?'"

"Frankly, business is slow."

"Hey, that's why I'm calling. Is your book in the library?"

"Why?" I asked.

"My wife won't let me buy any more books."

"He wanted a free book."

"That's awful," exclaimed Elmo. "Don't give your books away."

"Time to leave, Daddy," said Deidre.

"Time for our siesta." Dawn feigned a yawn.

Elmo stepped aside with a flourish to allow the Double D's to exit first.

❊ ❊ ❊

"Every day could be you last, so share your love far and wide with everyone you adore."

Amy Leigh Mercree

CHAPTER THIRTY-FOUR

"I Need A Friend."

"**M**ax, you look tired.Haven't you been sleeping?" Elmo asked. "Are you keeping something from me?"

"No, Elmo. Not that kind of tired. Perhaps, I should look for a part-time job. Matt keeps busy with the bookstore and editing my book."

"In other words, Matt is ghost writing your book," Elmo replied.

"In any case, I'd like to feel perky like you, Elmo."

"It ain't easy keeping up with two twenty-four-year-olds. Never a serious moment with that pair."

Max winked and looked to see if anyone was eavesdropping. "No mystery about that Elmo. I recall a children's story, a wonderful tale that only a person our age or nearing the end of life's journey might understand."

"Tell me more Max."

"Simply put, I feel like I am sitting on a tree stump in the middle of a clear-cut forest. I'm struggling to recall the missing tree."

"Shall I order coffee, Max? "

"Yes, make mine a Sassy with a double shot of caffeine."

"The drinks are on me," Elmo declared.

Max was astonished that Elmo was treating .

Elmo glanced at his mobile phone. " Oops! I'll have mine, 'to go.' The twins are paging me."

"But Elmo, I haven't finished my story. I need a friend."

"Duty calls, Max." Elmo abruptly left Jugz.

Max looked bewildered. He yawned and rubbed the back of his neck. When Elmo needed a friend, Max   was there for him. Elmo didn't return the favor.

Max confided, "Matt, no sense telling Elmo how I feel about something. It usually ends in an argument. Right or wrong, I end up apologizing."

"I know someone like that myself, Max. It's probably best to walk away, if you don't want the useless stress."

"That's a high price to pay. Is friendship supposed to be expensive?"

"I know it can be time-consuming," I said.

"So much for friendship," Max grumbled.

"Give me a call if you want to talk," I said.

"Thanks. I may take you up on it."

Max grabbed his 16-ounce Naughty with whipped cream, and headed home.

❋ ❋ ❋

"Friendship is born at that moment when one person says to another: 'What! You too? I thought I was the only one.'"

C.S. Lewis

CHAPTER THIRTY-FIVE

"Jam Session."

O rganizing a jam session is simple. Post a notice and musicians will come. I knew nothing about a jams session. Max shared some insights.

"For the uninitiated, Matt, a jam session is when musicians get together informally. Sometimes there are as many as ten or as few as two participants."

A jam session at Max's apartment could accommodate four, a keyboard, guitar, bass, and vocalist. Granted, they were squeezed into a tight space, but an abundance of alcohol compensated.

"My idea for a jam session was to have fun and ensure everyone had a chance to play. But Elmo insisted on a garage band. Right from the giddy-up, I knew garage band was destined to fail," Max said.

According to Max, Elmo kicked the jam session up a notch to a garage band. As Max put it, "A garage band rehearses in a garage because it can't afford to rent a studio."

Max could organize a jam session, but he lacked enthusiasm for a garage band even though that's how Bobby Sugar's band started. And with the addition of Dawn and Deidre there were six musicians with their favorite keys and chord progressions. "I lacked the up-front personality this newly formed band required. Plus, I didn't know how to say 'NO!'" admitted a dejected Max.

"Along with their innate talent, the musicians possessed strong personalities, more robust than mine. Looking back, it was never my intention to turn professional. Jamming was supposed to be fun, a plain vanilla garage band playing old-time rock 'n' roll."

Max imagined the group jamming on 24 cover songs - four chords and a simple twelve-bar structure - maybe some blues.

When word spread that Dawn and Deidre had joined the session, the phone rang off the hook with requests to join.

"It was my fault, Matt. I did some ad lib recruiting to the dismay of the guys."

"Despite everything - Bingo! - the band took on a life of its own and soon became an all-consuming preoccupation for me." Max looked chagrined.

Simply publishing a song list became a task. The lead sheets were posted by email or downloaded from one of the free Internet sites. Anyway, folks would arrive without music or bring their own arrangements. "What little enthusiasm I generated overruled my common sense."

"I was in trouble, Matt. Out of desperation, I called Bobby Sugar, my high school buddy."

Bobby told me, "Max, I haven't played my guitar in over twenty years. Miss Kitty and I lived in Muskego. That was bad enough, but gigging couldn't support three kids. And I didn't want Miss Kitty to go back to pole dancing. We packed up and moved to Florida. I found a full-time job at a boutique brewery. Miss Kitty and I have eight grandchildren. No more bands for me. I'm retired."

Bobby and Max talked about old times. As the conversation wound down, Bobby asked, "Max, why in the world do you want to play in a garage band? It will be the death of you. You don't have the personality. A band isn't a democracy. You gotta be thick-skinned."

"So you see Matt, Bobby was right. It's the old story. If it's free, it's advice; if you pay for it, it's counseling. I'd been there and done that. I didn't listen to Bobby and it proved painful."

❊ ❊ ❊

Often the hardest song to play well are the simple ones with just a few chords.
Marty Jourard

❉ ❉ ❉

Elmo French was determined the garage band would be a success. "Max, I produced some of the top groups LA has ever seen."

"Elmo was methodical. We rented a studio, rather than a garage. He paid for the studio time. He named the band - Climax."

"Elmo, I don't like the name. It sounds like we're pandering," Max complained.

"Relax Max. I'm not talking about an orgasm. In our case, the word Climax means a thrilling entertainment experience."

"Folks won't take it that way," Max warned.

"I'll leave it up to the public. As far as American culture goes, it's all perception and image. Few give a shit about substance. It's easier to promote a one word band - Climax - and let the chips fall where they may. I'm encouraging a fun evening, an escape to a simpler place in time, nostalgia and great entertainment for a bunch of geezers. Incidently, the term geezers has come under scrutiny. The gender-free posse prefers "geezer" be applicable to both curmudgeons and battleaxes."

"Elmo. how are we going to pay for all the expenses?"

"Don't worry. I'm footing the bill. I put up the money to pay royalties for screenshot projections of American Graffiti, too."

"Stop. Elmo, your plans are getting out of hand," I protested.

"Right now the baby boomers are in control. It's a male-dominated culture, but the women control the money. Max,

Americans are exhausted with all the media politics, I guess that's why so many are moving to Florida. Our audience hungers for the Fifties Oldies."

" But the Mickey Mouse Club just ain' t the same," Max said.

" We might as well make money off the choas," Elmo insisted.

✻ ✻ ✻

Elmo used his connections to get the band local gigs. We played small summer concerts to packed audiences.

Naturally, the Skipper sisters were the main attraction. With legs that just wouldn't quit, the shapely pair drew an excited audience. Dawn Skipper is no rival for Candy Dulfer on alto saxophone, but her stage presence worked wonders to arouse the crowd. The fans got their share of Oldies, but Deidre was caught up in Punk. Now and then Deidre got a solo. She played her heart out, and the crowd went wild. What a bass line. And the crowd didn't fight the feeling when the Skippers shook their booties.

As the summer progressed, Max began thinking about the group's future. As Max imagined, the simple jam session evolved into a garage band and finally a stage band. Max had no daydream of becoming an over-the-hill-rock star. On the other hand, Elmo was talking about a record contract and going on the road.

"Elmo, are you out of your mind? We aren't that good."

"A talented studio engineer can correct the vocals with vocoders and synthesizers. Fear not, my friend, the band will be in tune throughout the performance," Elmo assured Max.

Still, it wasn't the same. The guys had other responsibilities, too. They just weren't up to it. One by one, band members lost enthusiasm and drifted away. "We were down to five. And then there were three," Max told me. Every thing fell apart when the Skipper sisters quit.

Max avoided clashes over the equipment with the departing guys. Max owned the electronics.

Back in the day, Bobby Sugar told Max, "Own your own equipment." There is no misunderstanding. Leave it up to the group to assemble what's needed.

All-in-all, it was a learning experience. Max was determined, "Never again!"

"How does something as simple as jamming become so complicated?" I asked.

Here's the reason. The music, the booze, and pure fun- the rush - are addictive.

Playing two sets was no long enough. Max pushed the band for three.

On the down side, each gig or rehearsal required Max to pack his gear and jackass everything from his apartment, minus an elevator, to the various locations.

At the end of the night, Max had to pack up and lug his stuff home. And set it up again. One immense pain in the ass. So much for the band.

❋ ❋ ❋

"Remember when you're forming a band...the first thing you must consider is the guarantee that someday your band will break up. Consider your age, health, emotional state. Do you really need the stress? Oh, one other point: Think twice before you remarry your ex-wife."

Max Trotter

CHAPTER THIRTY-SIX

"Life Changed When the Music Died"

"Is there a good time to talk about my beloved Fairden and the pandemic? The lock-down and quarantines wounded Fairden's economy. Many of our service industry workers relocated. Several restaurants closed or operated on a modified schedule. The setback was nearly as great as the Great River Paper Mill closing and the Great Recession combined. Thankfully, the community is resilient and reviving.

Emma's Bookstore survived due to the devotion of my business partner, Sandra. I can still hear Sandra scolding me. "Matt you aren't carrying you share of the work."

Admittedly, we had a difficult time requiring our patrons to wear protective masks.

South Carolinians are still divided over social distancing and wearing protective masks. Some contend it has evolved into a red, blue, or purple political issue. The governor promises "No more lock-downs."

Nationwide polls found that many Americans believe Covid changed our lives forever. Some say we are now in a better place than we were early-on. Many also report feeling optimistic about their health, home life, and finances. Others disagree. And findings fluctuate from poll to poll.

❃ ❃ ❃

"Pandemic Loneliness"

"Elmo, I'm lonely," moaned Max.

"And to what do you attribute this feeling, my ruminating friend?" asked Max poking fun at his companion.

"Isolation. The increasing political divide in our nation. The split is finding its way into my neighborhood. "

"What's the purpose of talking about loneliness? Max you raise this theme continually. No one cares."

"With all this woke and cancel culture controversy, I'm leery of offending someone," Max confided.

I nodded in agreement. "Ever been to Wisconsin where it can be 35 degrees below zero?" I asked.

"No," Max replied.

"That's how I felt when my ex-wife got angry - really, pissed off. I knew I was in for it. Thanks to Liz, I've become a master at reading body language. Plus, I see a lot of T-shirt slogans, and AR-15 rifle tattoos browsing Emma's bookshelves. Those dudes are angry. They're lonely, and searching for friends."

"But why your bookstore, Matt?" Elmo asked.

"Books are a means to escape reality or discover like minded authors and readers. Maybe they just feel secure."

Max looked around and remarked, "A lot of lonely people here at Jugz, too."

"I don't feel lonely," said Elmo.

"That's because you are hunkering down with the Double D's," Max mumbled. "Nothing bothers that pair."

"Are the Skipper twins asymptomatic?"

"No. But they appear emotionally unaffected by confinement," replied Max.

"They have me. And I'm a notorious handful," Elmo responded with a touch of braggadocio and a wink.

Max waved his hand as though to negate Elmo's remark. "You're a legend in your own mind, Elmo," Max replied.

I could tell by the glimmer in Elmo's eyes that he was embellishing again.

"Suit yourself, my man. But I've developed a sleep disorder since the lockdown began. Dawn and Deidre are too demanding."

"That's what you say. According to Dawn, the twins have contracted cabin fever."

"Perhaps your right. Their behavior is insane. Dawn and Deidre turned from darts to ax throwing," Elmo sheepishly replied. "They force me to stand against the bedroom wall while they toss an ax at me from the bed. I've replaced the sheetrock with hardwood. My nerves are frayed."

"Elmo, are you nuts?"

"No! The twins are mesmerized by a video of Ed Ames teaching Johnny Carson how to throw a hatchet."

"You'll be sorry," I cautioned.

"How about you, Mr. Sublimation?" Elmo taunted Max.

"Sublimation? Are you accusing me of punching the clown?" asked Max.

I intervened before Elmo could respond. "Stop now before there's an argument. A gentleman never reveals the intimacies of his sex life," I insisted.

"There you go with that pretentious political correctness," said Elmo. "Don't go woke on me, Matt. I'm talking about Max's foibles."

"Elmo, this woke business is all bullshit, depending on which side of the line you're standing," I countered with an annoyed tinge. "From my perspective, subliminal sexual messaging in political ads targets males with fears of impotency. Now, can we move on before this bantering turns into an argument?"

"That's just like you, Matt. Why do you always call for a calm and reasoned approach?" Max aksed.

"Guys, woke means being conscious of racial discrimination in society. Elmo, you and I have covered this ground before. Your banter seems apropos to the current culture war skirmishes."

"Nonsense," barked Elmo.

"In a broader sense, woke could apply to all forms of societal injustice here and abroad."

"Like British-Irish history?" asked Elmo trying to draw Max into a meaningless debate.

"That's different," Max hastily responded.

"And why?" demanded Elmo.

"Because the British tyrannized the Irish. So it means just the opposite. Besides, I don't want to get into it." Max's complexion brightened as though he was going into a fight or flight mode.

"What's the opposite?" demanded Elmo.

Max didn't answer.

"All this cancel culture talk has me walking a tightrope," I admitted. "Let's change the subject before one of us says something we'll regret."

❋ ❋ ❋

I segued without skipping a beat. "Elmo your escapades with Dawn and Deidre sound like one of those housewives reality shows."

"Granted, I am an advocate of the stay-in-place notion thanks to the Skipper sister's companionship."

I pressed Elmo. "Don't you care about the Double D's' reputations?"

"Matt, I'm disappointed," said Elmo.

"Elmo, I recall you unashamedly shared a tidbit about a ménage à trois with those youngsters?"

"Videography is an art form. I'm opposed to pornography. But you bet your ass, my home is my sanctuary," Elmo retorted. "What goes on there stays there. Okay, every now and then, I shoot a few spontaneous video with my phone. I have a flair for producing and directing. I'll leave the screenwriting to you, Matt."

"Not me. I want no part of your productions," I insisted.

"As for Sylvia, I text her an impromptu clip now and then. I do it to make her jealous. What of it?" Elmo smiled.

"But you and Sylvia are estranged," I added.

Max, who had been extraordinarily quiet blurted, "That's disgusting, Elmo."

"Hey, don't blame me. Matt is writing this chapter of your pretentious memoir," Elmo protested. He pointed at me and asked, "Buddy, is Max's memoir becoming inappropriate? Be careful. It could be banned."

Max turned sullen. He looked at me. All I could do was shrug. I paused and tactfully responded. "Relax, with all the woke controversy who knows what is considered acceptable or unacceptable these days."

Just then Dawn and Deidre came upon the scene.

"Hey, here come the girls. Not a word about their reputations or my home movies," said Elmo.

"Guys what's the controversy about?" asked Deidre. I could hear you guys barking as we walked in.

"It's true," said Dawn. "Folks come to Jugz for a bit of serenity."

"Oh, we are discussing Max's memoir. The controversy about woke."

Deidre laughed. "Are you shitting me?"

Admittedly, I was shocked by Deidre's response.

Then she said, "Someone has to have the balls to say the controversy really amounts to money and power. It's greed. If you don't like what someone is saying, you accuse them of being 'woke.' It's like wrapping yourself in the flag. I asked a guy at the beach how come he had a beach towel that looked like our nation's flag? I told him that was disrespectful. He said to go 'F' myself. Think about it; the towel was probably made by child laborers. It's all about greed and power. We are an angry nation. Blame it on Covid, I guess."

Deidre joined Dawn at the counter and ordered a Sassy.

"What the hell is bugging her?" asked Elmo. "I noticed she's becoming arrogant and temperamental. Dawn, too. They are so assertive and opinionated. Where are they getting these ideas?"

I decided not to walk through that door and returned to our discussion of Max's memoir.

"Max, best we prepare several press releases to give you enough 'shimmy.' So far, your story is mostly good fun with brief moments of seriousness."

"Do you think the book should have two or three different cover blurbs?" asked Max.

"Why three?"

"I have reds to right of me and blues to the left of me. I'm kinda stuck in the middle with purple."

"Matt, after Deidre's little tantrum, I'm questioning my hunger for companionship – the feeling, the sensations, the touch, and aura of a woman."

"Nonsense," said Elmo.

"Max, you are only human and that's what I hope to convey in your memoir. But not salaciously."

"Max, you're a hard man to please," said Elmo.

Max looked at me and said, "Elmo may be right, Matt. At the end of the day, what is happiness?"

Elmo interrupted. "You're filling Max's head with foolishness, Matt. He's bound to get hurt. Look in the mirror. Like most writers, you are a moody, selfish, and romantic dreamer. Romantics can't let go of a daydream."

"No way, Elmo," I responded. "You have expectations rather than anticipations. I'm just the opposite. We've talked about this before."

"Stop arguing," Max demanded. "All I'm asking for is a sensible woman. Hard working. One who loves me passionately and never complains."

"If you can find a rational woman, marry her," Elmo replied as he sauntered to the counter to discover what was bugging Deidre.

* * *

In the meantime, Max's feelings of loneliness and depression mirrored the challenges many Americans faced, except for Elmo and the Skipper twins.

Suprisingly, Max told me he felt ambivalent about what the future might hold.

Max and a friend tried jamming via Zoom. Something was missing. Max gave a couple of impromptu sidewalk solo performances, too. Car horns honked. A driver shouted "Bravo!" A fender bender and fear of contributory negligence ended the concerts.

Thanks to Sandra, Emma's Bookstore remained opened, on a limited schedule. I had few financial worries and more free time, still my preoccupation with completing Max's faux memoir intensified.

She used the downtime to rearrange the store inventory. I grew to appreciate her presence and input more than ever. I did notice a tiny twinge in my chest each time I spoke with Sandra.

* * *

But as you may imagine, the pandemic did not stop our dynamic quartet - Max, Elmo, and the Double D's - from innovatively surviving the situation.

While Jugz curtailed in-house service, the "drive thru" window remained open. Jugz's parking lot became the social watering hole for Fairden. Tailgating prevailed. Folks brought their beach chairs and sipped their java. Political discourse and gossip prevailed.

❋ ❋ ❋

"The Parking Lot Dispute."

My phone rang. "Matt, join us at Jugz's parking lot. My treat," said Max. I hoped he would arrive on time. No dice. So I sipped the eight-ounce mocha Teaser that I purchased and eavesdropped on an unsuspecting couple's spicey conversation.

About ten feet in front of me, two men were facing off over what I suspected was an ideological donnybrook. Can you imagine a steel-toed, brawny right-winger gesturing to fight a skinny, rabid liberal wearing a "Free Hugs" T-shirt, pink shorts and flip-flops?

A crowd gathered. Mr. Pink Shorts claimed that an anonymous billionaire donated millions to the Park Service in return for a tax deduction and the understanding that his profile would be added to Mount Rushmore.

"That's fake news," shouted the guy in the steel-toed boots. "You pinkos are all alike. Next, you'll be telling us God is dead."

"Hell no!" shouted Mr. Pink Shorts. "She's alive."

Hearing this, an outraged bystander dropped his cup and sauntered toward Mr. Pink Shorts. "Get out of the parking lot. We don't want no trade unionists around here."

Luckily for the skinny liberal, Max, Elmo and the Skipper sisters arrived just in the nick of time. As luck would have it, tonight, the saucy Double D's were showing off their street-savvy lingerie and braless ensembles. An old guy sipping Fire Ball shouted "huba huba."

❋ ❋ ❋

"The Skippers calmed the raucous crowd. Serenity prevailed.

"Ladies, you saved the evening. I am proud of you," Elmo said. "I don't mind spending a few hundred bucks on diamond studded masks when you respond so conscientiously. "

Dawn and Deidre exchanged slack expressions as though to say, "That's okay by us, but what's wrong with Elmo?"

Deidre held her finger to her lips and whispered, "Don't look a gift horse in the mouth."

❊ ❊ ❊

"Hysteria plus cruelty is a recipe for violence."
David French

CHAPTER THIRTY-SEVEN

"The T-Shirt Quandary"

I t was tough finding a parking space in Jugz's parking lot. I searched for Max, Elmo, and the twins. They usually sat in the round with medical masks hanging from one ear. Of course, the Double D's' jewel studded masks cost Elmo a pretty penny.

Surprisingly, tonight Elmo sat alone on an uncomfortable sand chair. I winced at the sight of Elmo's contorted torso.

Max and the Double D's were nowhere in sight. I walked to the window and ordered a 6-ounce Teaser with a dab of whipped cream and walked over to where Elmo was seated.

"Tough finding a parking space."

"I agree," said Elmo. "Fairden is a retirement community. So, fifty percent of the parking spaces should be designated Handicap Parking. On the other hand, as the owner of Jugz, I'd protest littering my parking lot with Handicap Accessible signs.

"Elmo, Federal guidelines require a Handicap Parking sign be placed a minimum of 60 inches above the surface. I saw an inattentive pedestrian walk into one," I remarked.

"It's not a problem for me, Matt. But those unpainted concrete curb stops are a disaster," Elmo replied.

"Elmo you appear preoccupied," I told him.

"I'm sorry Matt. Didn't mean to spoil your evening." Elmo looked at me and blurted, "Matt, the Skipper sisters charged a grand on my credit card for eighty printed T-shirts."

"What's printed on the T-shirts?"

"Asymptomatic!" Elmo pounded his fists against his thighs. "They plan to give the shirts away. It's their contribution to social distancing."

"I see your point, Elmo. Who in their right mind will tell the world they are asymptomatic?" I asked.

"Telling the truth is insane. Who cares? That's like a T-shirt emblazoned, *STD*," said Max.

"Those precocious blondes are always stirring the pot. But this is taking a bad situation to an extreme," I said.

Elmo shrugged "My social life will be ruined."

Elmo grew silent and gazed into his coffee. Then he murmured, "The twins threatened to call off our trip to Cabo if I cancelled the T-shirt order."

"Elmo, at some point you must put your foot down. Be tough," I urged. "Sex isn't everything."

"That's easier said than done, Matt."

I was desperate to find someone to back me up. I picked up my cell phone and asked, "Siri, is sex the answer to everything."

"I don't have the answer to that," Siri replied.

"Are you kidding? Siri's been "woked," grumbled Elmo.

"Elmo, Siri is software. Siri is no longer a woman. Apple took away her gender."

"What? Isn't messing with gender illegal?" Elmo tore the phone from my hand and shouted, "Siri, who's your Daddy?"

"I don't have a family tree. But I have a pretty great file directory." The voice was the same, but the answers were different.

Elmo fumed. "By god, not only did they delete her

gender, but they deleted her emotions, too."

" Calm down Elmo. How a person describes their gender is a personal choice."

"Thank god, no one will ever change the Skippers."
"Why?"

"Shopping revs them up. Whether it's boutique shopping or bargain hunting, Dawn and Deidre get it on."

"Elmo, that can't be real. Its all in your mind," I told him.

"The twins equate an afternoon's shopping to prolonged foreplay. The more they spend, the more playful they are at home. And that's not my imagination running away with me. Believe me. When it comes to aphrodisiacs, never underestimate the power of shopping."

"So what's the bottom line, Elmo?"

"I pretend not to need sex or their vivacious tastes when they come home from shopping. In turn, the Double D's crave my attention and you know how they get it. I let them shop!"

"Gosh Elmo. The Skippers can create one heck of   a catch - 22."

✻ ✻ ✻

"From now on I'm thinking only of me."
Joseph Heller, Catch-22

CHAPTER THIRTY-EIGHT

"Is This The Beginning or Is It The End?"

I telephoned Max the other morning. "Hey, I haven't seen Elmo for weeks. I know the Skipper sisters aren't living with him. What's up?"

"Matt, I have some sad news about our frolicking Elmo."

"What happened. Max?"

"This morning I drove over to Elmo's apartment. He moved to the far side of town since his separation from Sylvia. I called, texted, and posted 'Call me!' on his Facebook page. I knocked on the apartment door, but Elmo didn't answer. Then in desperation I began pounding the door with my fist and shouted, "I know you're in there Elmo."

"A neighbor greeted me. She asked, 'No answer?' I saw Mr. French snatch the newspaper off the doormat a few minutes ago.'"

"I pounded on the door,again. I shouted 'Elmo, I know you're in there. It's me, Max. Open the door or I'm calling 911.' I heard the chain lock clatter and turn as Elmo grappled with the doorknob."

"The door partially opened, Elmo peered up at me. The dark circles under his eyes and his disheveled hair sounded the alarm."

"What do you want?" Elmo stammered.

"What do you mean…what do I want? I feared something had happened to you."

"I'm OK. Sorry for the trouble. I'll catch up with you," Elmo grumbled giving me the bum's rush.

"Something's wrong," I said, and abruptly pushed my

way inside.

The place smelled like a Dumpster. The stench came from the small kitchenette. Imagine a mile-high stack of dirty dishes and an overflowing garbage can. An assortment of dirty pots graced the stovetop.

"Elmo, what the hell is going on here? Look at you. You're a mess."

"I'm busy, Max!"

"Too busy to shower? You look awful and smell worse." *I regret scolding him.*

Just as Elmo started to explain, the sound of bursting bubbles caught my attention.

"Was that your cell phone?" I asked.

"I don't hear anything," he mumbled.

"There it is again."

I walked across the room and found the iPad I had given Elmo a couple of months ago.

"It's a notification on your tablet. It's *Words With Friends.* I know because Ann plays the game."

"Give me that!" Elmo blurted out as he seized the tablet and turned away. "That's private."

"You're right. I'm sorry."

The last six months had been tough for Elmo. I thought the iPad would provide a distraction; maybe he'd email friends or get on Facebook, anything to lift his spirits. Elmo seemed to be suffering from depression. Depression hurts, especially if you've lost two of the most precious things in your life. In Elmo's case our band fell apart. And the following week Sylvia exchanged Elmo for a spiritual journey to India.

❋ ❋ ❋

Enter Matt Nagle.

Let's pause for a minute. There is emotional tension attached to Max finding Elmo in crisis. Ann, Max's estranged wife, cautioned me that Max is a great storyteller, but he sometimes he divulges too much information.

Nevertheless, I could tell that Max felt Elmo's pain. Elmo needed to exorcise his demons. Some folks bang on pots and pans. Elmo locked himself away but it wasn't working. Max is no psychotherapist. What else could he do but listen to Elmo's rendition - the drama, the emotion, turmoil, and agony - of the band splitting up?

Okay, let's return to Max helping Elmo with his dilemma.

✳ ✳ ✳

"You've got to get out of this apartment, Elmo."

I opened the patio door to the tiny balcony overlooking the apartment parking lot and a nearby sewage aeration field. The acrid stench from the sewage plant waft into Elmo's apartment. I closed the door and turned to Elmo.

"Matt, look at me. I have a lifetime pension, health care, and money in the bank. And most of all, my prostate functions. I'm depressed! Silvia's gone. My kids live all over the country. They haven't spoken with me in years. All I've got is Words With Friends and Facebook."

I felt a judgmental scowl cross my face. "My god, Elmo, what's this?" Tacked to the far wall were dozens of text messages and e-mail exchanges along with a tally for Words With Friends games with Sylvia.

I threw my hands into the air. "Computer games aren't reality, Elmo."

Elmo gazed at his tablet for a few seconds. "I'm not addicted to Words With Friends," he protested.

"From where I stand it looks like you're glued to that iPad."

"I'm not."

"Look at you. Every time that thing sounds, you shake. It's got a hold on you."

"You don't understand," Elmo pleaded. "It's Sylvia. I miss her."

"Elmo, it's a fantasy. This is the second time she's abandoned you for that yogi in India. Haven't you had enough?"

"Why?"

Elmo slumped into his worn recliner. His iPad slipped to the floor. He cupped his face and sobbed.

"Constantly checking your iPad for a text or words from Sylvia is a delusion, Elmo."

"Max, I can't go to the bathroom without my iPad," Elmo confessed.

"Elmo you are depressed. You are a successful record producer. A fashion plate. Women love you. Men envy you. Get hold of yourself, man."

"I can't, Max. I'm alone. I fear abandonment."

"Elmo, the band was destined to break up. We weren't the Rolling Stones. We were a garage band. People change. The band went out of control. I wasn't cut out to be a stage band rocker. You knew that from the beginning. Once you put Dawn and Deidre out front, they took over. And that's not my imagination running away with me. How can you miss the drama?"

"I do," Elmo replied with a moan.

"You know what they say?" I asked.

"No, Max. What do they say?"

Elmo's response caught me off guard. I had no idea what to respond. I hesitated, cleared my throat, stalling to come up with something. And then I remembered the day, the hour, the minute and second when the band crashed. "Bands break up. Most of the time it's over a woman or a chord. We joked about the possibility the first time we jammed. Remember?"

"Kinda."

"There are a million other reasons. Like the difference between a riff and a rift," I said.

Elmo shrugged and turned away. He didn't want to hear it.

"As for your marriage, how many guys remarry their first wife? Did you remarry Sylvia to recover your money or because you love her?"

"Maybe both," Elmo said.

"You and Sylvia are continually at each other's throats."

"You're right. Sylvia and I just can't talk about anything meaningful. It always turns into an argument. We have a list of off-limits topics, especially when it comes to passion and intimacy. I felt we were on the way to a reconciliation, Max. And now look at this mess. All because I blurted out 'Sylvia had a face lift.'"

"Perhaps that was the proverbial cap on the tube of toothpaste thing, just like the band," I responded.

"Wait a minute. Tell me about the face-lift? What the hell does that have to do with Sylvia leaving?"

Elmo pulled himself to the edge of his leather recliner and replied, "We were at dinner with our friends, Tom and Gloria. Tom commented that people are living longer. 'Gloria acts like 70 is the new 39 for woman.' That didn't go over well."

Elmo paused.

"Then what happened?" I asked.

Gloria asked, "Do you think I should have a face lift?'"

I replied, and regret every word, "Sylvia had facial injections. They cost over a thousand bucks. Left bruises, too. Can you tell any difference?"

Max looked astonished. "Are you kidding?"

Sad-faced Elmo said, "As usual my mouth out-ran my brain, if I still have one. It was an innocent remark. Sylvia added it to her 'I'll never forgive you' list; the straw that broke the camel's back."

I could picture Elmo and Sylvia when they arrived at

Elmo's apartment later that evening. You guessed it.

"I hoped Sylvia would spend the night. I was getting undressed when the brawl broke-out," Elmo whimpered.

Suddenly Elmo's arms began to flail. "Sylvia exploded. She raged and came at me. Sylvia's an Amazon. Look at me, Max. I'm five-one maybe four in my Bugarri loafers. Just like that…bam! She tossed me onto the balcony. Max are you afraid of death?"

"I guess." I shrugged. "I've thought about it."

Elmo rushed to the patio door and pulled-back the drapes. "You don't know Sylvia." He glared at me. That night, I thought I was going to die." Elmo was reliving a nightmare.

"Max, I heard the building superintendent shout from the parking lot, 'Mr. French, get some clothes on. This is a respectable apartment complex.' I feared he would call the cops."

Elmo voice was gravelly. I walked to the kitchenette and filled a glass with water. He was sweating like a pig.

"I can't live without Sylvia," he moaned.

I was beginning to understand his quandary. *Sometimes we do something for so long that we don't see there's any other way.*

"Here, Elmo drink this."

A knock on the apartment door interrupted Elmo's story and gave me a breather.

"Mr. French, are you okay?" It was the building superintendent.

"Good morning. I'm Max Trotter, Mr. French's friend. Elmo told me about the unfortunate balcony incident."

Elmo warily stood behind me. "Sorry about the disruption," Elmo mumbled to the superintendent.

"You and Mrs. French created a circus, I'm sorry to say. You two were louder than usual. I encountered Mrs. French dragging something down the stairs. I hid in a doorway. I though it might be your dead body, but it was only that stuffed dog of yours. She struggled to put it in the trunk of her car. Mrs. French set off the car alarm, too. Caused quite a commotion. Tenants complained. I didn't call the cops because I know Mrs. French is a difficult woman."

Elmo pointed to the empty corner by the door. "Scotty's gone, too," he sobbed.

"Elmo, it's a stuffed dog."

"Maybe to you, but Scotty was a friend. I just couldn't say goodbye. Damn Sylvia. She's so vindictive."

Elmo looked old, tired, and tattered. He seemed to be on the verge of a breakdown. Perhaps he was already there.

"Gosh, Mr. French, I didn't mean to upset you. I'll get out of here." said the superintendent.

After a few minutes I decided to leave, too.

"Elmo. I'll be back tomorrow. Take a shower and get this place cleaned." I knew it wasn't that simple.

"Elmo you are not alone. There must be a Twelve Step detox program for Words With Friends addicts. But let's take it one day at a time. I'm your friend. When you need me, just call and I'll be here."

❋ ❋ ❋

"It's tough when you miss musicians you used to perform with. But if you miss them, it means you were very lucky. You had amazing people in your life to share your passion for music with. Not everyone gets that."
Musicians Unite

CHAPTER THIRTY-NINE

"The Comfort Pony"

Several months following Sylvia's departure to India she moved in with her yogi, Veer Shevade. Sylvia's affinity for the supernatural began when she met the yogi, AKA Buster Bragg, a former cage wrestler.

Sylvia's latest obsession, Veer Shevade, claims clairvoyant powers. The self-proclaimed shaman, hosts a weekly podcast, *You and Your Other Self*.

On a positive note, Sylvia's estrangement meant Elmo could return to his Sweet Water home.

"Matt, Elmo complains about loneliness," said Max. To please Sylvia, Elmo tried to break his addiction to the Skippers. I can't figure it out. Sylvia doesn't give a shit."

"Is he happier now?" I asked.

"Is Elmo ever happy? For now, Dawn and Deidre are domiciled at 1202 Dixie Lane in Sweet Water."

"And Elmo still isn't happy?" I asked. "He needs to keep busy. Elmo needs a pet."

"I love animals. How about a puppy. A puppy requires lots of attention just like the Double D's."

"I've got it ," I said. "Let's buy him a couple of pet miniature horses."

"Ponies?"

"No, Max. A miniature horse is not a pony. A pony is a small horse with a thick neck, stumpy legs, and a thick mane and tail. A miniature horse is smaller than a pony or even a Great Dane."

"Agreed. But I'll leave the research to you," Max agreed.

* * *

To my delight, I found a pair of miniature horses for sale.

"Why two miniature horses, Matt?"

"The breeder convinced me that miniature horses, not unlike Elmo French, are frequently subject to loneliness. So, I purchased the pair."

The two miniature horses were delivered to the Sweet Water address several days later.

Elmo named the male horse Red and the female he called Blue. The horses silently wandered Elmo's enclosed backyard.

Unfortunately, as author Ernest Hemingway noted, "Good deeds often lead to disaster." In other words, for every action, there are unintended consequences.

As usual Dawn and Deidre were constantly bickering. Their catfights were turning into Sweet Water mythology. The yard fence failed to baffle the curiosity and eyebrow flashing of the ever increasing numbers of dog-walkers strolling by.

More intrusive yet, a neighbor knelt at his bedroom window snapping digital shots of the topless twins sunbathing and romping in the pool. Suddenly, Red and Blue caught his eye.

"That son of a bitch, Elmo French. He thinks he's beyond the homeowner's rules," the voyeur told his wife.

The wife, a disgruntled member of the Community Enforcement Committee, immediately notified management and the River County Animal Control.

"The guy has two miniature horses in his backyard. The county rule calls for one-half acre per horse. He's got two horses on a half-acre."

The following day Elmo was served with a county summons and an HOA violation notice.

* * *

Elmo presented his case at the next monthly County Zoning Board Of Appeals.

"Red and Blue are miniature horses. They shelter in my garage. Please don't make me give one of the horses away," Elmo pleaded.

"Could you please stand, Mr. French?"

The diminutive Elmo shouted, "I am standing."

"Well then, stand on your chair, or come forward to the microphone."" After several attempts to balance on the cushioned seat, Elmo approached the microphone.

"Mr. French, you can board the miniature horses at a stable," said the Chairman.

"Mr. Chairman, my wife and I don't want Mr. French keeping the horses on property. I would like you to review this video as evidence." The surly neighbor walked forward and handed his cell phone to the Chairman.

After careful review the red-faced Chairman said,"Sir, this is some great footage." He slammed the gavel and called the members into executive session.

Elmo returned to his seat. He knew the odds were against keeping the cherished horses. Meanwhile, Dawn and Deidre exited the meeting hall and were flirting with a police officer monitoring the entrance door. Those two have an affinity for men in uniform.

The dishonorable neighbor garnished his video with shots of the twins romping in the pool. Once the all -male board gained their composure and returned to the room. The meeting reconvened.

The Chairman slammed the gavel again. "Mr. French, do you have anything to add?"

"Yes, I love Red and Blue," Elmo replied with tears in his

eyes.

The Board members denied Elmo's appeal. "Quite honestly, Mr. French, the County Code stipulates one-half acre per horse."

"But they are tiny horses, Mr. Chairman," Elmo pleaded.

"It doesn't matter. Red and Blue are horses, Mr. French. And you know what they say - 'A horse is a horse, of course, Mr. French."

The Chairman slammed his gavel again - "Next case!"

* * *

"No one can talk to a horse of course."

The theme song from Mister Ed.

CHAPTER FORTY

"Black Friday"

The Covid lockdown drastically altered many lifestyles. "The question remains, Would Covid restrictions end a unique American holiday event?"

"Thanksgiving?" I asked.

"No, not Thanksgiving. I'm talking about Black Friday," Max replied. "Elmo invested a small fortune on the return of Black Friday."

According to Elmo, the pandemic had changed many Americans' cognitive view of the world. People prefer misery over happiness. The contentious political atmosphere, often called the great American political divide, threatens traditional retail shopping. Retailers depend on Black Friday's survival just like politicians depend on the culture wars.

"Matt, Americans are unhappy, unchallenged, and bored. They long for adventure, yet fear straying from the safety of their living rooms," said Max.

"Is this another one of Elmo French's schemes? What's the plan?" I asked.

"Please don't let the cat out of the bag. Elmo will kill me. He's promoting what he calls The Black Friday Adventure."

I grimaced. "Elmo never settles for simplicity in thought or form. He goes for the gusto."

"Nevertheless, his latest project may find a market: *The Black Friday Keepsake Video*," Max insisted.

According to Max, Elmo's idea brings new meaning to the word "vicarious."

Max went on to explain that for a fee, Elmo would provide an unforgettable Black Friday experience at the retail store of your choice. Elmo planned to retain a string of retired professional wrestlers and NFL cast-offs to act as proxy shoppers. The big lugs would be wearing body cameras.

Shoppers would endure the violence, cold weather, and painful twelve-hour wait on your behalf. When the doors open, you would rush in. All from the comfort of your home.

Want a TV, computer, or refrigerator? Your proxy is certain to make the purchase. And your bonus? You'll receive a lifetime memory of a personalized video thumb drive as a keepsake of the insanity.

"I'm starting to get the picture, Max," I replied.

"Well, there you have it, Matt. Elmo is the idea man. I do the dirty work. While Elmo is wrestling with the "Double D's on Beckwith Beach in the Caribbean, I'm recruiting hulks for a proxy shopping spree."

"It isn't fair," I said. "It seems that every year Elmo comes up with some creative idea, but leaves all the work to you."

"I agree. Last year it was the Christmas Hug scheme. Can you imagine receiving a coupon from a distant love, redeemable for one great big hug?"

"Duh. I know. Who wants a hug coupon for Christmas?" Matt shrugged.

"I'd like a real hug," I replied.

"Walmart thought a Christmas hug booth was a bum idea. They weren't coughing-up an travel expense account.

Max's cell phone sounded. It was a call from Elmo.

"That was my cue to leave."

"Not so soon, Matt. There's one more scheme."

Max's hand trembled.

"Max. What are you doing? You're spilling coffee all over."

* * *

"I just heard the news. I'm beside myself. "

"What news?"

"Your recent novel. It's fabricated, embellished... a pack of lies. You concocted the whole story. Won't that detract from my anthology?"

"It's a novel, Max."

"Elmo is orchestrating the promotion."

"What promotion?"

"A book club coloring book edition of your novel *Brandi Barton*."

"Is this another one of his Ponzi capers? He can't do that. I hold the copyright. That's insane. He never discussed coloring books with me."

"Brace yourself, Matt. Elmo is giving away a box of gray crayons and reading glasses with each purchase. *Brandi Barton* is loaded with colorful scenes," said Max.

"True. And many libraries have banned *Brandi Barton*," I added.

"Elmo's counting on even more outrage with all the cancel-culture and political correctness controversies, to boost sales," said Max.

"It's a popular novel at Emma's Bookstore and on the Internet. I don't need a coloring book promotion," I protested.

"Please don't tell Elmo I told you," Max replied.

❋ ❋ ❋

The following week Elmo returned from the Caribbean.

"Elmo, you promised me we were going to the Post Office. You do this all the time. Now we are standing in front of Jugz collecting signatures for your absurd idea."

"Relax Max. I only need a few more signatures to make this petition look impressive."

"Elmo, who wants Black Friday moved to Thanksgiving Day morning? Folks are watching the parade or a football game."

"Retail merchants want it. I want to promote my Black Friday Video Adventure. If the idea flies, I'll expand the video to cover families enjoying Thanksgiving dinner."

"Elmo, I recall a Thanksgiving when there were plenty of fixings to go round. Mother served a great meal. We didn't have video games back then. We watched the Macy's Parade in the morning and after dinner we watched King Kong on TV."

"We went out to dinner on Thanksgiving," Elmo recalled. The old man loved Horn and Hardart Automats in New York City. Every Sunday morning my mother would force me to watch The Horn and Hardart Children's Hour. Yuck!

My mother thought the prepackaged food was crummy, but she hated to cook.

I got a kick out of staring through a tiny glass window at a rotating drum with shelves of food. I'd drop a token in the slot. *Presto!* I'd open the door and grab my pumpkin pie. And my old man didn't care what I ate as long as I didn't spend more than a buck-fifty."

"I remember the Children's Hour, said Max. "But when Thanksgiving rolled around, I loved Temptation Friday, the day after Thanksgiving. I considered myself a good Catholic boy, who would never break the Church's decree of a meatless Friday. But I lusted for a sliced turkey sandwich on rye with lettuce, cranberry sauce and mayo dripping between the slices. I shamelessly took the first forbidden mouthful that almost rivaled my sweet heart's first kiss."

❅ ❅ ❅

A few days later Max met Elmo at Jugz.

"Elmo are you alright?" Max asked.

"Yes, thanks Max. Sometimes I feel harried keeping pace with Dawn's and Deidre's shopping lifestyle."

Max realized that the Double D's and Sylvia's dalliances were straining Elmo's sanity and his discretionary funds. Elmo's pension and his trust fund were evaporating. Luckily, Elmo and the twins seemed to have a trove of marketing schemes. The Skipper twins were his promotional gold mine. Here is an example.

Dawn suggested a unique party icebreaker - Covid martini stirrers. "Daddy, we recycle used Covid test sticks."

"I found this used stick in the garbage. It's positive, but that doesn't matter. This is a demonstration," said Deidre as she displayed the carelessly discarded Covid test with her gloved hand.

"They make great three-olive martini 'swirlers' and distinctive party conversation starters," Dawn added.

"And swirling beats meaningless conversation," added Deidre.

"I hate to burst your bubble ladies, but your idea isn't going to fly," Elmo insisted.

"Why?" asked Dawn.

"Can you imagine Dumpster diving behind CVS for negative strips?" Elmo laughed.

❄ ❄ ❄

"When I was a kid, national holidays were special with parades and stuff like that. We always got the day off from school. I loved Washington's Birthday because it is my birthday, too," said Elmo.

"Wow! And Max Trotter was born on the Fourth of

July," said Deidre.

"Most states celebrated George Washington's birthday by closing schools and other municipal services," Elmo explained.

"So people could shop?"

"No, Dawn. Anyway, Abe Lincoln isn't too popular. Neither are paid vacation days.Congress couldn't get enough votes to declare a national Lincoln holiday. Today, nobody knows and who cares about George Washington or Abraham Lincoln"

"Why, daddy?" asked Dawn.

"Because Presidents' Day is a national shopping day, nearly as frenzied as Black Friday or Tax-Free Weekends in South Carolina."

"Daddy will there ever be a National Diazepam Day?" asked Deidre.

Elmo scowled. I doubt it darling. But I'll bet there will be a National CBD/Hemp Day. I can imagine the T-shirt slogan - 'Got Hemp?'"

❋ ❋ ❋

" There are eleven annual U.S. federal holidays plus Inauguration Day."

CHAPTER FORTY-ONE

"More Holiday Shopping?"

Elmo and Max sat at a corner table of Jugz sipping java. "Max I need gift suggestions for the twins."

"I doubt you need my assistance with your holiday list, Elmo. We have different tastes when it comes to gifts. Plus, I'm on a fixed income."

"True. This year, I'm purchasing several big-budget items plus a few tasteful intimate items to spice up the relationships."

"Intimate? I'm uncomfortable shopping at Victoria's Secret. I'd buy anything just to get out of there,"Max confessed.

"Oh Max, get a hold on yourself. I take my time shopping. But I'm not talking about lingerie, Max."

"Elmo, when it comes to *50 Shades of Grey*, I'm out," said Max. He raised both hands shoulders-high as though to stop an on-coming freight train.

"I'm not talking about the proclivities of pain and pleasure either, Max. Just simple fun."

Elmo pointed to a newspaper article. "It's rumored that Walmart is selling adult sexual wellness toys on their website." He handed the clipping to Max.

"Never."

"Oh, yes. Their rivals do it. This isn't fake news. The twins told me." Elmo protested. "I read the story in the financial section."

"Do Dawn and Deidre indulge?" Max innocently inquired.

"An excellent question, my inquisitive friend. I didn't ask

187

the Double D's for fear of embarrassing them. They can throw a tantrum."

"Elmo, I doubt those two would decline discussing the topic."

"Can you keep a secret?"

Before Max nodded agreement, Elmo blurted, "I checked their bedrooms. What a collection!" Elmo's eye's bulged. "I know a vibrator when I see one, but what in the hell are the rest of those gadgets?"

Max shrugged. "I have no idea. But, my friend, you just damaged your 'know-it-all' bragging rights."

"Certainly not, Max. The ladies have their 'needs.' Look at it this way. Do athletes train? Do bands rehearse? Excuse me for a minute Max. I'll be right back."

When Elmo returned Max asked, "What took you so long?"

"To save money, Jugz converted to hand dryers rather than paper. Not my favorite. But as Jugz's owner, I must put profit ahead of my personal preferences. So, I dried my hands on my shirt and waited a few minutes for the next patron to open the restroom door. I don't want to touch the door knob."

"Elmo, you are a character. Aren't you going to sit down?"

"No, Max."

"Elmo, you haven't finished your chai tea latte Teaser. Where are you going?"

"Walmart Max. Want to come along?"

"Not today, Elmo. I get blue at holiday time.I'll sit here and finish my coffee."

"I get sad as Christmas approaches," said Elmo.

"I miss the conversations and jokes as we sat around our family's kitchen table. Living in a funeral home didn't stifle the laughter and good feelings as the holidays approached. Although Christmas was a bit tense."

"Times have changed," said Elmo.

"I agree. Today, folks don't sit together at the kitchen table. They graze and load their paper plate and find a comfortable chair. Next thing you know everyone is surfing the Internet."

"Probably for the best," Elmo remarked. "People no longer converse. They pick arguments."

Max nodded in agreement.

"It's rumored that the government implanted tracking devices in turkeys weighing more than eleven pounds to enforce Covid regulations."

"Are you kidding?" asked Max.

"It's another way of checking families complied with social distancing. You can't feed more than eight people on an eleven-pound turkey."

❊ ❊ ❊

"Max, I don't mean to pry, but earlier you remarked about being blue at holiday time. Christmas is supposed to bring anticipation and fulfilled wishes; lots of stories about the shining eyes of children. Those expectations are killers when you live in a funeral home. Some Christmases were better than others, but the worst was the freezing Christmas morning my goldfish died."

"How did you handle those sad holidays," I asked.

"Matt, do you recall my stories about Bobby Sugar's band?"

"Sure," I replied.

"I played piano. Mom and dad bought an old upright piano; probably the best gift I ever received."

Max explained that before the piano could cross Serenity's threshold, Uncle John insisted on two conditions.

The piano would be delivered to Serenity's third floor,

called the attic. It was freezing in the winter and sweltering in the summer.

And second, Uncle John insisted that Max would learn to play Uncle John's favorite song, Amazing Grace.

"Why?" I asked.

Max shrugged. "Who knows? It's a secret Uncle John took with him to the crematorium."

"But, I practiced every day to please my parents, and placate Uncle John. After a while practice became a habit."

I was a bit mystified, by Max's explanation. I imagined that playing the piano might fill hours of loneliness. Then again, while the funeral home's routine would appear stifling, it was a reality that prepared Max for the final chapters of his life.

"Only an aficionado will understand how rock 'n' roll expresses life's longings and reinvigorates one's spirit," Max said.

* * *

Max, and Elmo are characters. Max still loves his piano. And Elmo?

Elmo once told me he envisions himself seated in a recording studio control booth adjusting the sliders on a massive sound board. "Nothing like the Wall of Sound, a brilliant engineer, and the Wrecking Crew working your session."

I fear to think that for these two septuagenarians, the road ahead boils down to crossing a bridge from what we were to who we are, today. Get busy gentlemen. Time is slip-sliding away.

CHAPTER FORTY-TWO

"Loving Comfort"

Max spent his formative years living in Uncle John's funeral home. Max's parents moved to a modest home in Patchogue when Bob Finch, a family friend, purchased the establishment.

One day Bob called Max. "Max my sister moved to Bluffton. I'll be visiting for a week. I was hoping to drive to Fairden and discuss a few proposed changes to Uncle John's funeral home."

"Bob, it's great to hear from you. Looking forward to seeing you."

A few days later Bob met with Max at Jugz.

"Your Uncle John always felt pressured to come up with a new sales pitch. Back then, radio ads were less expensive than TV commercials. Running a family funeral home is a killer. The large franchises are moving in. And get this. They're selling caskets."

"I'm not sure how I can help you," Max said.

"I have a meeting at the bank next week. I want to upgrade my facility. I thought you might help me prepare," Bob said.

"Of course... shoot."

"I want my establishment to retain Uncle John's casual, yet traditional, ambiance; more than a place where the dead are prepared for burial or cremation. Nevertheless, I need some upgrades and innovations."

Bob's comments caught Max by suprise. *Uncle John must be turning in his grave.*

"To start, I'm changing the name to 'Loving Comfort.' Locals will always call it 'Uncle John's,' but the older generation is moving to Florida where woke supposedly dies. That concept of death troubles me."

"It's political, Bob. You got it wrong."

"I hope so. The story I heard was about some guy named Woke. I don't pay too much attention to the news. He was headed to Florida to die. Who knows?"

"I understand Bob. If someone is going to die I'd rather see them pass away in Patchogue so you get the business."

"Exactly. Just the same, I need younger clients, too. I want to bury or cremate villagers without reference to political affiliation and ballyhoo. Every human being deserves a non-partisan, shame-free funeral. Don't misunderstand me. We're sophisticated, but in a simple way; no fuss."

"I understand. So,why change the name, Bob?"

"Loving Comfort sounds reassuring in these uncertain times."

"What else?" asked Max.

"The building's design is dated. I plan to modernize. Social distancing demands innovation. Who knows what catastrophes lurk in the shadows waiting to bight us in the ass. I want a contingency in place. My chapel isn't large enough to meet the CDC's recommendations. It's tough to view the departed in a casket from five or six feet away, even with overhead mirrors and monitors. My first change will be the 'drive through visitation.' You stay in your car and ride by a picture window. I've designed a revolving casket platform."

"A what?" Max couldn't hide his perplexed reaction.

Bob responded by opening a folder and handing Max a newspaper clipping and pencil sketches.

"A Virginia-based funeral home is installing video cameras, so family and friends can view services online via the Internet. Also, grieving families may choose to have their loved ones' ashes made into rings, pendants, and keepsakes. My two favorites are the commemorative golf ball and sportsmen's shotgun shells. You drive that golf ball and it explodes midair spreading ashes over the fairway."

Bob anxiously awaited Max's response.

Max paused and took a couple of sips of his whipped cream covered Sassy. "This is quite a departure from Uncle John's approach," Max said as he wiped whipped cream from his nose. But I do know one fellow who might buy into it for his departure."

"Uncle John recognized the funeral business is changing," Bob said.

"He did?" I asked.

"Sure. I loved Uncle John's idea to recycle pacemakers. And don't forget his plan to salvage titanium nuts, bolts, and prosthesis. He ran a great gray-market business in Brazil."

"You've got a point," Max said nodding in agreement. "I recall when he paid me to trap mice in the mortuary. Is that it, Bob?" Max asked.

"Not quite. Here's the twist. On the average, funeral homes enjoy a 200 percent to 400 percent markup on casket sales. Most families are feeling an economic pinch, but too proud not to purchase an ornate casket."

Max nodded in agreement. So, what's your solution?"

"The mail order do-it-yourself casket. No cutting or gluing. I recommend buying one now and having it on hand when the need arises."

Max gave sigh and a grimace of pain.

"I'm including a red, white, and blue casket cover for the first 100 orders."

"Will the Church approve a red, white, and blue pall?"

"Oops. I've done it again, Max. Should I also make one in red, white, and purple?" Max.

"Relax, Bob. Forget I asked."

"There's one more modernization, but I'm not sure the folks back home are ready for it."

"What is it?" Max asked bracing for the unexpected. Bob pulled out another clipping from his folder. "Here's the kicker." Bob's beamed as he handed the clipping to Max."

"A New Orleans funeral establishment gained notoriety yesterday with its premier viewing of Irma Smith. Ms. Smith, a lifelong football fan, died last week. Ms. Smiht spent her service sitting at a table amid miniature football helmets, with a can of beer in one hand and a cigarette between her fingers, just as she had spent many of her living days."

"Bob surely you're joking."
"No. I'm already getting calls," Bob said."I need to enlarge my funeral home to accommodate these requests. Uncle John's chapel is way too small." Bob lifted his 10-ounce Teaser latte and looked around to be sure no one was eavesdropping. "I am going for the gusto," he said.
Max looked puzzled. "There's more?"
"The ultimate diorama: A viewing of Tom, our beloved paramedic, displayed behind the wheel of his ambulance."
"Bob get hold of yourself. Isn't Tom is still alive?"
"Of course, he is," Bob said. "And that's the point. Tom purchased my new preplanning package. He's been texting me selfies all week."
Max downed the remaining drops of his Sassy. "Wow. Time flies. I must run. You may be on to something, Bob. One last idea. Why not have an very merry unbirthday party? It could be a fun time for friends and family to attend a prepaid funeral rehearsal."
"I'm not sure about that one, Max."

"Good luck with your bank presentation. You'll get the loan." Max gave a thumbs-up.
"Thanks for listening, Max. I'll call to tell you how the meeting went," said Bob. "Hey, next time the Sassy is on me."

* * *

"Is your prepaid funeral ready for the 'new normal?'"
Robert "Bob" Finch

CHAPTER FORTY-THREE

"Libraries Have Changed."

After his surreal meeting with the funeral director Bob Finch, Max needed to unclutter his mind. Max called Laura several times and left messages. Laura didn't return his calls. He still missed her.

Later that day Max met me at Jugz.

"Matt, I wish Laura was here."

What choice did Max have but to accept the inevitable? *It is what it is.*

"Matt, I guess it was unfair of me to treat Laura like she was my therapist rather than a friend. I skipped the friendship part and went right to... Max paused.

"What's wrong?"

"I'm not sure where Laura and I were in our relationship."

"Go easy on yourself, Max."

Max scratched his head and said, "I'm friggin' Humpty Dumpty. My life's in bits and pieces. I expected Laura to put me back together again. "She's gone, Matt. Simple as that. She's gone."

I tried to warn Max to *tread lightly*. The real world can be depressing. The fictional world is so much more fun than the real world. Laura Finley is an exciting woman in her own right. I feared the *real* Laura might break Max's heart. And she did. I regret creating Laura. I guess I'll have to buy Max a ticket back to reality.

* * *

It wasn't long before Max sought sanctuary in the community library, just as he did in high school. Max waited in line until the library opened and scrambled to find a seat at a cloistered table behind the stacks.

Max's notebooks are filled with anecdotes pointing to one conclusion, public libraries have become a sanctuary for the homeless.

Contemporary librarians are not only reference resources, but in many cases they fill the role of an on-hand social worker. Max hightlighted a few brief anecdotes.

One fellow, dressed in a corduroy jacket and colorful ascot appointed Max the guardian of his two-wheeled grocery cart jammed with his life's possessions. The man's battered guitar case rested an arm's length away from Max. "Please keep an eye on this. I'll be back in a while," the man requested.

Another patron pursued a conversation with the microfiche machine.

A thirty-year-old card dealer, lost her job in Atlantic City. She lived in her Toyota Corolla.

The library was as busy as an airport terminal, serving residents, vacationers, the weary, homeless, and troubled. And then there was Dan Prunes.

❊ ❊ ❊

Hi: It's me again, Matt Nagle.

I apologize for interrupting Max's story, but I'm confused about some of the terminology.

I read that there are nearly six hundred thousand homeless people living in the United States. Homeless, houseless, unhoused, or unsheltered. Which term is correct? Fairden is a small retirement community. We don't have shelters for the homeless.

Nearby Millcreek Commons recently leveled a homeless encampment.

I'll sit this one out and let Max relate this episode in his own words.

❊ ❊ ❊

Max first encountered the fellow on a rainy morning at the library.

"Sorry about hogging the men's room, but I felt really crummy. My name is Dan, Dan Prunes."

"Pleased to meet you, Dan. I'm Max Trotter."

Max looked perplexed as he strained to focus on the conversation. Live and learn Max wrote in his journal:

"Taking a sponge bath in the men's room is a bit odd. The scene reminded me of living under Uncle John's roof.

Uncle John was a born water-conscious conservationist. Hot baths for the Trotters were reserved for the weekends. Uncle John argued that he needed the hot water for the embalming process. He was recycling brown water before Rachel Carson published *Silent Spring*. A hose attached to the washing machine irrigated the lawn and garden. As I recall, folks laughed, but it worked."

At first sight Max assumed Dan was homeless. That wasn't the case.

As Dan tells it, "A while back, Betty, my wife, passed away. I was devastated. That's the downside of a happy marriage."

A few months passed, and Dan decided to sell the house, lock, stock, and barrel; time to move on. Dan, a frugal man, banked the bulk of the proceeds from the house sale, purchased a converted van, and circled his neighborhood for a goodbye. And that's how Dan ended-up in Fairden.

"Where are you headed, Dan?"

"I haven't the slightest idea, Max. I own my van and I have money in the bank. I love libraries. Free Internet. I park overnight at Walmart. A couple of times a month I stay at a motel. My cell phone takes care of the rest. Life is simple."

That evening, Max Googled Dan's name on the Internet. Nada! I called a friend whose hobby was geneology.

"I can find dried plums in every corner of the planet, yet, I can't find a trace of Dan Prunes or the Prunes family," Max told his friend.

His friend explained the downside of geneology this way. "It's sad, Max, but not all the great contributions of men and women named 'Prunes' were recorded by historians."

Max invited Dan to join him at Jugz. Over an apple fritter, Max told Dan about his interest in geneology, but didn't reveal the search for Dan's family name.

"I'll bet you won't find the Prunes family," Dan replied. "We Prunes are very uncool, and unsexy. So who cares?"

Their conversation lasted about an hour.

"I'm moving on, today," Dan said as the two men walked into the parking lot.

They shook hands. Max wished Dan good luck and waved as his truck headed along Front Street toward the Bypass.

Ever since that day Max can't say "prunes" without smiling.

CHAPTER FORTY-FOUR

"The Prevailing Theme"

One evening Max, Elmo, and I met for coffee at Jugz's parking lot. I wanted to revisit Max's concerns about isolation and loneliness, the prevailing theme of his many anecdotes.

"Matt, doesn't it seem strange that wherever you go, there I am?" Elmo asked.

"That goes for you too, Max. Don't you have other friends? Loneliness is all you talk about," Elmo insisted.

"I disagree Elmo. Max isn't the only one expressing depression or loneliness," I said. "Many residents living in my condo complain of feeling lonely. Max attributed his feelings of isolation to the increasing political divide in our nation.The split is finding its way into my neighborhood, too," I added.

"What's the use of even talking about loneliness? No one cares. And with all this 'woke' and cancel culture controversy, I'm afraid of offending someone," Max said in hushed tones.

"I agreed. Ever been to Wisconsin where it can be 35 degrees below zero?"

"No," Max replied.

"When my ex-wife got pissed off at me, that's how it felt. Speaking of anger, I've become a master at reading body language, T-Shirt slogans, and AR-15 rifle tattoos. There are a lot of lonely and unhappy people in Fairden. And they wander into Emma's Bookstore."

"I don't feel lonely," said Elmo.

"That's because you are hunkering down with the

Double D's," Max mumbled.

Max waved his hand as though to negate Elmo's remark. "I've heard all this before, Elmo. You are embellishing, again."

"Suit yourself, my man. But I've savored the Skipper twins' impulsive passion, and insatiable appetites. A lesser man would find it impossible to satisfy their desires," Elmo assured his companions.

"That's not what Dawn told me. The twins have contracted cabin fever."

Foolishly, the conversation turned serious and I allowed myself to be drawn in.

"Max, you ruminate about world events. What can you do about whether China threatens our economy or climate change? Plus, you can't let go of your morbid childhood in the funeral home," Elmo cruelly chastised.

"Before we get down to business could you answer one question?" I asked Elmo.

"Of course. Shoot," Elmo defiantly replied.

"What's your attraction to tall women? The twins are five-eight. Sylvia, your estranged wife, is six feet tall. Elmo, you stand just about five-one in elevator shoes."

"The truth?"

"Yes."

To this point, Dawn and Deidre sat next to Elmo without adding to the conversation.

Elmo looked at the twins and said, "Assist me ladies."

"It's not Elmo's height that attracts us," said Dawn. "It's Elmo's confidence.

"And don't let me forget to mention his money," said fearless Deidre.

"Max, I'm not attracted to tall women. They are attracted by my genuine self-confidence, masculinity, and intelligence. The taller they are the more they crave me. What they see on the outside counts. But what you don't see is monumental," said Elmo with a wink. "Max, you're too timid around secure women."

 Max frowned.

"Fine, Max. Let's hear your story."

"You never take me seriously, Elmo," Max protested. "You scold me in front of my friends. Friends don't do that to friends."

"Hold on, Max. Could we save these concerns for another time?"

"Sure, Elmo, but what's your rush? You justify your rudeness by claiming that I'm too sensitive. That's not the case. I wanted to tell you what I learned from meeting Dan Prunes," Max replied.

"The homeless guy?" asked Elmo. "Nobody in their right mind would admit their name is Prunes. Would you go to a gastroenterologist named Bowels? I don't think so. Tell Prunes to change his name. Other than that, it sounds like a great story."

"Dan Prunes is a flesh and blood human being," Max said.

"Surely you're joking. Listen to my dilemma," Elmo shouted.

Max's complexion flushed. He was upset. Elmo paid no attention to Max's stunned expression. "Ladies, will you excuse us for a minute?" Once the Skippers were out of earshot, Elmo whispered, "Sorry for yelling at you, Max. The twins are driving me crazy."

"How?"

"Deidre wants a sports car. And Dawn is so precocious. Implants, implants, implants! That's all she talks about. But how can I deny them?"

Max the people pleaser replied, "I'm sorry, Elmo. Please let me pay for your coffee."

Max forgives too easily. He needs to carry a grudge.

"Time to go, Daddy," Deidre said.

"Duty calls, Max. Let's talk about Dan Prunes next time."

❋ ❋ ❋

"Perhaps one did not want to be loved so much as to be understood."
George Orwell, 1984

CHAPTER FORTY-FIVE

"The Security Bubble"

One morning, Max called. "Matt, Elmo and I are out for a walk in Deepmarsh Village. Elmo is hosting a Zoom party today, at 4:20."

"Thanks Max, but 4:20 is too early for me to start partying. I'm at work. The store closes at 6:oo. It's Sandra's day off."

I heard Elmo shouting in the background, "Matt, you old fart, it's never too early to party. The Skippers will be there, too."

Shame on me for not standing by my convictions. I folded. Business was slow that afternoon. I walked to my office, and opened a bottle of pino noir. At 4:10, I switched on the store surveillance cameras.

At exactly 4:20, a Zoom invitation appeared on my computer screen. It's a miracle how computers work. Elmo joined us from his master bedroom. He turned the camera toward the attached deck.

"Hi boys," shouted Dawn and Deidre as they climbed out of the hot tub and scampered into the master bedroom.

Faster than you can say 'Jack be nimble," the pair grabbed Elmo and pulled him into the air. Regrettably Deidre lost her grip and Elmo crashed to the floor like a bowling ball.

"Come on, Daddy. Let's give it one more try."

"Absolutely not," protested the stunned Elmo. He walked to the end of the huge heart-shaped bed, climbed the bed steps and smiled. With that Elmo pulled a remote from his pocket. Music filled the room. "Let's boogie-down" he shouted.

"What do you think of the twins' dance moves, Matt?"

Before I could answer Max yelled, "Calm down ladies, our session is turning into a melee."

"You'd better not be taping this Max," warned Elmo. Dawn jumped off the bed. She returned carrying a bottle of Ruinart and three champagne flutes. She poured a glass for Elmo and the sisters returned to the hot tub.

Elmo sat on the edge of the bed.

"The gang seems to be holding up well," I remarked.

"Not really," Elmo replied. He groused about the usual stuff as he closed the sliding doors to the deck. The twins could not hear the conversation.

"The twins are too demanding," he moaned. "They are constantly purchasing on Amazon. They enjoy flirting with the delivery man." Elmo sounded jealous.

I suggested Max help Elmo create a list of diversions to occupy the twins.

❋ ❋ ❋

Several days later, Elmo called to thank me. He ordered a three-dimensional printer and plastic sheets made from recycled soft drink bottles.

"I'm designing an inflatable plastic bubble for the twins. The pesky pair can climb inside the bubble, and go for a stroll, without violating Deepmarsh homeowners' rules."

I cautioned Elmo that it is important to pump fresh air into the bubble to prevent possible suffocation.

"You've got to see the twins in the bubble, Matt," Elmo bragged.

A few days later I accepted another invitation and it was a hilarious display of devotion. Max and Elmo raced behind the bubble pulling a little red wagon carrying a cylinder of compressed air.

* * *

Max and I ran into the twins last evening at Jugz. It was a rare occasion when Elmo wasn't with them.

"Where's Elmo?" I inquired.

"Elmo is preoccupied. He is determined to design a biosphere to keep folks safe from the virus. You got him started on this craziness, Max."

"Not me." Max said.

"I watched you two in the bubble. You're awesome. You can meander the community. But isn't it awkward having people gawking at you?" I asked.

"It's rather restrictive, Matt. On our next roam through Deepmarsh we will wear body cameras," said Dawn.

"Elmo wants us to produce a reality video, The Real Bubble Girls of Deepmarsh Village."

"Give that idea some thought. Wearing a body camera may attract unwanted attention," I cautioned.

"This is America, Matt." Deidre said.

Max responded, "Everybody likes democracy until they don't. So watch your ass."

Deidre turned, stretched and pretended to peek at her posterior. "I can't do it. You guys will have to keep an eye on it for me."

❊   ❊   ❊

I recall when Elmo moved to Deepmarsh Village. I was surprised since Deepmarsh Village is known for its owners' rules and regulations. At the time, Sylvia's lawyer, L.G. Trustme, demanded that Elmo vacate the Sweet Water mansion.

"Don't do it," Max argued. "Shout sanctuary and plant your flag. It's your home, too."

"Read this," Elmo handed Max a letter. "L.G. is forcing me to abandon my favorite Lazy Boy, 'Big Blue.' Sylvia wants me to grovel. No sense arguing. L.G. knows no pity. L.G. is crueler and more hard- hard - hard - hearted than Sylvia."

Elmo wiped away a few tears. Elmo stammers when he becomes anxious. I'm not poking fun at stammering, but that's Elmo. Nevertheless, I have trouble with watching someone cry.

Bugs Bunny always pointed a finger at his archenemy, Elmer Fudd - "I hate to see a grown man cry."

Getting back to Sylvia, and the fiendish, L.G.

"Screw Sylvia. Oops! The heck with Sylvia," Max shouted.

"Guys, I'm not so sure about L.G. Trustme. It's rumored that manipulation and fear are her stock-in-trade. Be careful," I warned.

"Hmm. I remember the first time Sylvia and I divorced. L.G. came up with a bunch of clever, but devasting moves."

"Elmo, you've been put on notice," I cautioned.

"Okey dokey, Matt. Whatever you say," Elmo nodded in agreement.

But our spirited duo wanted Big Blue.

"I'll show Sylvia and her lawyer." said Elmo

Elmo and Max rented a van and around midnight they rescued Big Blue. Big Blue now rests in Elmo's living room.

"Sylvia can't get her claws on Big Blue now. Deepmarsh Village is gated," Elmo assured me.

* * *

One afternoon the Skipper sisters invited me to watch them in the bubble. Actually, they needed someone to help Max pull the little red wagon. Elmo was preoccupied with his 3-D Printer.

I noticed the girls weren't wearing slippers.

Bubble integrity demands occupants have bare feet. Accordingly, the Skippers' casual attire raises the ire and concern of residents when it comes to the propriety of "thongs."

Max cautioned, "Listen ladies, Deepmarsh rules prohibit thongs in the common areas. Don't you think we should tell Elmo before you two slip into those thongs, ladies? Elmo signed a rental agreement."

"Nonsense Matt," said Dawn.

The adventurous Skipper sisters paid no heed to my warnings and a few minutes later they rolled away. Max and I ran after them pulling the little red wagon with the fresh air supply. "Slow down ladies," I implored them. Nevertheless, off they went.

A few minutes, an alert watchman spotted the bubble and called for a "hot pursuit."

The Double D's panicked, turned left rather than right. The bubble, minus the fresh air supply, headed down Bay Street like a snowball escaping the fires of hell. The spherical cavity kept picking up speed. Max and I could not keep up. The bubble was out of control.

Suddenly the bubble crashed into one of the last community pine trees. Thud! The bubble burst like a rogue Chinese surveillance ballon. It made a weird slow-release flatulence sound. Max called it a fart and swore he could smell intestinal gas. Did it matter? No!What mattered was the collapsing blob trapping the twins.

The pursuing watchmen grabbed their knives and began cutting the bubble into shreds fearing the trapped Skippers might suffocate. I feared that in their exuberance the two might slice the twins.

The flood of bystanders sounded like howling "timber wolves."

Regrettably, in their rush to rescue Dawn and Deidre, the watchmen overlooked an innocent pedestrian who was pushing her dog in a stroller. In the nick of time, her left foot protruded from under the collapsed bubble. Both the owner and dog survived.

Getting back to the twins. There is no Deepmarsh rule prohibiting wandering the streets in a bubble. On the other hand, the scantily clothed Skippers received a stern reprimand from the homeowners' association about wearing thongs in amenities and common areas.

"There you have it," Deidre protested. "Elmo's obsession with keeping us safe is stirring up trouble."

"Talk with him, Matt. We don't want another bubble," the Double D's pleaded.

"Elmo is obsessed with bubbles," said Dawn. "I don't

mind residing in a privileged community. But now we know first-hand that bubbles burst, Matt. You gotta help us."

Deidre hugged me. It was the first time I had seen her cry.

I assured the twins, "Everything will be okay. I've learned that everything in life is temporary, even sadness."

❊ ❊ ❊

What's happened to our nation when you just can't be who you are?

Anonymous

CHAPTER FORTY-SIX

"Max Trotter on Growing Old (er)"

I dropped by Jugz last night for some time-out and a Sassy. It never fails. In walked Elmo French.

"Hey Matt."

"Hello, Elmo. Where are the twins?"

"They will be along."

Since Sylvia left Elmo, he had become increasingly dependent, if not addicted, to the Skipper sisters. Granted, they are a voluptuous, sensual, and indulgent pair. However, I've tried to warn Elmo about his heart condition. He laughs.

"Relax, Matt. I reviewed a few intimate questions with my doctor. Did you know that sex is a contributing factor in less than one percent of heart attacks; less dangerous than a horror movie. And she talked about sex."

"Not 'her' or 'she,' Elmo. Your primary care physician is Dr. Ann Phani. That's the politically correct way of putting it."

"Hear me out, Matt. Dr. Phani recommended not lying on my back during sex which realistically I'm incapable of doing. Dr. Phani shared a secret, Matt."

"This should be a good one, Elmo," I replied.

"A lot of sexual disfunction is caused by unhappiness. Sylvia constantly complains, but not the twins."

I smiled. *Dr. Phani might be on to something.*

"As for the twins, they're happiest when they have my credit card," said Elmo. "And Dr. Phani contends that when the twins are happy, I should feel overjoyed. Dr. Phani makes a lot of sense."

THE POLITICALLY INCORRECT MAX TROTTER

"Let's focus on you, Matt, my researching maniac. So, what finds you at Jugz? More research for your next novel? You and your damned research. You should be enjoying your freedom. Have you finished Max's memoir?"

I looked at Elmo and thought not as much about his questions, but his motivation. *Elmo is constantly fishing for something to stir the pot.*

"I don't want to appear unfriendly, but Sandra is watching the store. I popped in for two Sassies to go. As for Max's faux memoir, it's nearly complete," I said.

"And how is Max helping?" asked Elmo.

"By staying out of the way. At first, Max claimed he has no regrets with the manuscript. Sure enough, few days later he called and told me to add this and delete that. His author's alterations are perplexing. On the other hand, Max keeps telling me that perhaps he would have done many things differently. I can fabricate a corrected past, but then Max wouldn't be Max. That's not how life works."

Elmo swallowed the last drop of his java. "Who knows? Can't look back now. For me, the road ahead is narrower and shorter, if you know what I mean. Dr. Phani reminded me, 'Elmo there is enough stuff to worry about today. Stop worrying about tomorrow. At your age it's a gamble.'" Elmo laughed.

Elmo's remark puzzled me. Suddenly he was turning into a stoic. No way. Just then our conversation was interrupted.

"Look who's here," said Elmo as he waved. "The Skipper twins are in the house."

"Matt, I had a couple of setbacks in the record

business. They seem like a breeze compared with Sylvia's machinations."

"Elmo, I feel the same way about my situation, minus the twins."

The Skippers joined us.

"So what are you two gentlemen discussing?" asked Deidre.

"Growing old," said Elmo.

"Not old. Older, Daddy," said Dawn.

"Have it your way. But, you twenty-four-year-olds can't imagine what it feels like to be approaching seventy-five."

"And we don't want to," said Dawn turning to Deidre.

"Dawn is right. Why talk about it? Time will tell," said Deidre.

"Time will tell?" I asked. *Rarely does time tell anything except age.* "There's a difference between getting old and aging."

"Does living longer bring happiness?" asked Deidre.

I was stunned. *Good question.*

"I like the twins calling me Daddy. Kind of a reverence for my age." Elmo winked and smiled.

I grimaced. *Elmo, you're revolting. Elmo relishes making sly innuendos.*

Elmo looked right at me. "Think what you like Matt, but you are making a mistake by overlooking Sandra Holt."

"What does Sandra have to do with this? Sandra's my business partner Elmo. I learned a long time ago to never mix business and pleasure."

"Then buy her out." Elmo bellowed and let out one of his boisterous laughs.

Deidre pushed away from the table. "Daddy you need a refill."

A few minutes later, Deidre in her usual fashion, nudged Elmo and placed his drink on the table.

I sensed that Deidres' sexy interaction with Elmo stirred Dawn's jealousy.

"How are the book sales, Matt? " I turned around to discover Max had arrived. *Have you noticed that wherever I go Max shows up?*

"Great I replied." There were a number of eavesdropping customers and I hoped to pique their curiosity. However, concerning my finances I discreetly replied, "Authors must be thick-skinned, but last night I was wounded."

"How so?" Max asked.

"A long-time college friend asked about my book sales. Who tells the truth about books sales? I told him my books were selling well thanks to the Covid lockdown."

"Is your current novel in the library?"

"I don't know. You live in Maine. Why?"

"My wife won't let me buy any more books."

"He wanted a free book?" asked Elmo.

I nodded and murmured, "Yes."

"Don't give him a book. Let him buy it. Two things you don't give away - your love and your books," Max replied.

Elmo yawned. "It's bedtime for these two," said Elmo tugging at Dawn and Deidre. He laughed and began humming an Elvis favorite - "Steamroller Blues."

"I must run too, " said Max.

❋ ❋ ❋

"The things one desires are often the things we find unattainable. They can really cause confusion in our lives."
Anonymous

CHAPTER FORTY-SEVEN

"The Parking Lot At Sunset"

I met Max, Elmo, and the twins at Jugz parking lot last evening. It was chilly but the sunset over the river was amazing.

Folks bring beach chairs. I can't figure it out, but Dawn and Deidre enjoy sand chairs. The macadam in no way feels like sand. I suspect the sisters like to relax and stretch after being confined in the house for most of the day. When it comes to deliberately flexing in a sand chair the Double D's are tops."

"Why do we always meet at Jugz?" Deidre asked.

"I'll bet it's because this a is faux memoir, and all the interesting scenes take place here," I joked.

"Oh, I figured we met here because Elmo owns Jugz and he is making big bucks from these mini conventions. The parking lot is packed," replied Max.

"Nice talk my cynical friend. You have such a suspicious mind. Brace yourself. Next week Jugz is sponsoring the Tuesday Night Cruise-In. Nothing serious. No judges. Everything is casual and fun. And Jugz's 'Naughty' will be the star attraction."

"Don't you need a city permit?" I asked.

"It's my parking lot. Dawn and Deidre will direct cars to the drive Drive Thru window. I'm not charging admission. Parking is free with the purchase of a 16 ounce Naughty in a Jugz Dream Car Mug to go. The way I see it, a Dream Car Mug plus the twins directing traffic are the answers to any man's nostalgic wish fulfillment."

"What about the women, Elmo?"

"Max, you sly fox. I'm not stepping through that door."

"But the parking lot is so uncomfortable," Deidre complained. "I urged Elmo to build a sandbox for Dawn and me, a kinda make believe beach."

"And what did he say?" I asked.

"No. Sandboxes attract fleas and cat fouling lets off a disgusting smell," said Dawn.

Deidre shrugged. "Maybe Elmo is right."

Turning to Max, I asked, "Max, why do you look so frazzled?"

"Someone posted my picture on Facebook for Fathers' Day. As if I don't have enough to deal with."

"Calm down Max," I said. His face broke out in a rash.

"What if my kids see that? They rarely call me as it is."

"Relax Max," said Elmo. "Some joker is always messing with me on Tik Tok. I've never been to China."

Of course, the precocious Double D's were bickering. This time over Dawn's assertion that the identical twins had different fathers.

Elmo checked to see if a nearby couple may have overheard the twins' squabbling.

The twins relaxed in their sand chairs and stretched to their fullest as they pretended to be at the beach. Their contortions soon proved to be a distraction for patrons at the drive-thru window. Drivers honked their horns and howled. But the Double D's persisted.

Suddenly, I heard a thundering crash and looked toward the drive-thru line. A car and pickup truck had collided. The car's driver exited his vehicle and pointed at the Skipper sisters.

"Hey, you two. Put on some clothes."

Undetered, Deidre laughed and tossed the guy the

bird.

The driver shouted an obscenity. Deidre leaped to her feet and jogged across the parking lot toward the guy. Dawn ran after her.

The driver jumped back into his car. He was trapped in the drive-thru line. Deidre ran in front of the car and mooned the guy. The crowd cheered.

Someone had called the cops. A police car's siren blared as it raced into the parking lot and squealed to a stop blocking the drive-thru exit. A second squad car arrived. The cops directed the two drivers to pull forward. Both drivers were searched and ticketed.

"That fearless pair sure can get a rise out of this crowd," cheered a bystander pointing to the Skippers. Sadly, no one had stepped forward to help the sisters.

❋ ❋ ❋

Seconds later, someone set off an argument about the pickup's wheels.

One guy called the truck a mall crawler, a less than kind description.

His comment provoked a Mega Mud Truck enthusiast from the opposite camp. "Watch your mouth you egg-sucking asshole." The truck lover hauled-off and punched the critic right in the nose. I guess he didn't like the other guy's take on the out-of -proportion pickup tires.

People bicker and fight over just about anything these days. There's always people in the crowd calling someone else a liar. It isn't worth getting involved. Whether it's pickup trucks or ice cream flavors, someone is bound to be offended. And it's politically incorrect for me to tell the bickerers to "Get over it."

❅ ❅ ❅

Elmo waved and called, "Ladies, you are causing quite a ruckus.

"Daddy, Deidre had me sweatin' like a sinner in chuch. I didn't like the looks of that guy."

"I agree. Never trust a guy in a pickup truck that doesn't have a gun rack and a dog," said Elmo.

Max was about to stir the pot. "I heard you created a big stir last week when you drove down the boat ramp. The marina water is so unhealthy." Max's comment was cruel.

"What happened?" I asked, but suspected the answer.

"The boat ramp needs signage," Deidre insisted.

"Hog wash," said Elmo. "I've warned you a million times to use caution on foggy nights."

"It's the pandemic's fault. Our lives will never be the same," Dawn grumbled.

"Daddy, you own Jugz. We need a walk-up window. The Maserati is too low to the ground. The drive-thru guy nearly climbs out the window to hand us our drinks."

"I'll bet," said Elmo. "Gentlemen, what do you think about the young man's intentions?"

Max and I smirked, but said nothing.

"I'm not going to install a special window to accommodate your Maserati. That's a frivolous expense. The Governor promised that the long walk through the pandemic tunnel is about to end. Any day now, Jugz will swing open its doors and life will return to normal."

❅ ❅ ❅

By now you see why I enjoy the cozy parking lot get-togethers with the fearless foursome. Nevertheless there were times when I felt uncomfortable. I'm struggling with the meaning of "covfefe." Elmo first mentioned covfefe.

"POTUS set off a flutter over the 'covfefe debate,'" Elmo told me.

"Covfefe?" Max asked.

"Come on Max. You're pulling my leg. Covfefe has received so much negative press. It's gone viral" Elmo replied.

"What does it mean?" Max asked.

"Only a small circle of people know exactly what it means. I tried to beat POTUS to the punch and trade mark covfere for Jugzjava.com. No dice. Every President worth his salt holds the honor of adding a new term to the American lexicon," said Elmo.

"President Harding coined the term 'normalcy,'" I said.

"Who else?" Deidre challenged.

I looked at Deidre. I felt the challenge in her voice. *Deidre can be a pain in the ass.*

"Here goes." I began checking off the Presidents. "Harding coined another term, 'bloviation.' Washington – 'administration.' Jefferson –'lengthily and belittle.' Teddy Roosevelt – 'lunatic fringe and muckraker.'"

Deidre suppressed her surprise and growled for me to "Get a life."

Elmo asked, "Matt, what's with you and Deidre arguing over a covfefe?"

I shrugged. I try to avoid an argument with Deidre by walking away. It didn't matter. Max took over.

"Never heard of covfefe," Max replied.

"Matt probably knows," said Elmo.

"Oh, get out Daddy," said Deidre. She enjoyed

provoking me. "Matt is no genius."

"I don't care what people say. I bet 'covfefe' is a secret code word," said Dawn.

Elmo paused and scratched his head, a sure sign he was contemplating a response. "I recall the coded messages from Little Orphan Annie when I was a kid," said Elmo.

"You can't remember what you ate for breakfast," said Deidre. Everyone laughed.

"Drink your Ovaltine! I waited weeks for my secret decoder," bragged Elmo.

"What a rip-off," Max complained. "I agree with Ralphie, the kid in *A Christmas Story*. The secret message was nothing more than a crummy comercial," he added.

I wasn't about to admit the details of my favorite childhood fantasy to this crowd, so I made something up. I confessed, "there was a time when I wanted to be a leader in my gang, too. So, I drank instant Ovaltine everyday for rocket power. Confidentially, I also owned a Captain Midnight Secret Squadron decoder, too."

Getting back to the subject at hand, Elmo was about to fire a 50-caliber remark that would outdo a Jugz Espresso Double shot. It was bound to echo in every café around the world.

"Covfefe means…Jugz forever!" Elmo shouted. "Damn if only I could trade mark covfefe."

"Holy smokes, Elmo. That's brilliant. But what about POTUS?" Max declared in amazement.

"I can have my own definition," replied Elmo.

"Someone is sure to argue you are politically incorrect. Americans are so litigious."

"So catch this politically incorrect napalm bomb." All eyes turned to Elmo French. Without warning Elmo, the world's champion at clouding an issue, changed topics like turning off a light switch.

"Americans are spoiled. They whimper and demand

at the slightest inconvenience," Elmo vented.

I looked at Max. *Where's Elmo going with this?*

"Forty million households, that's fifty-three percent of occupied American households, live inside a homeowners association. The majority have one pandemic liberation mantra: 'OPEN THE POOL.'"

"That explains the T-shirt I spotted on a shopper in Publix," said Max.

"What did it say?" asked Deidre.

"TAKE BACK OUR COMMUNITY!" Max said.

"Max, will things get worse?" asked Dawn.

"Yes. Americans are angry, and they want to vent."

"Damn right," said Elmo. "Some of our best traditions are disappearing thanks to Dr. Fauci and the gang of four at the CDC."

"The Gang of Four? Isn't that an English punk band from the 1970s? Are they still around?" asked Deidre.

I replied, "I don't know about punk bands, but I agree with Fauci. Wear the confounded mask. Fauci puzzles me. The country hasn't faced a pandemic since the Spanish flu. Fauci's got the science and I agree that science isn't perfect. Still, he's a national punching bag."

"Daddy, can we change the subject?" asked Deidre. Her playful fingers tiptoed along Elmo's thigh.

"Social distancing is a lot of bunk, Matt," Elmo shot back. "Thanks to Fauci, millions of Americans feel threatened by a Covid home test. It's a menace to the spontaneous afternoon 'quickie'. Despite Fauci the twins and I still enjoy our afternoon delight."

"Elmo, the quickie is out. The slow burn is in, especially for septuagenarians," Max said.

An incensed Elmo fluttered his arms as though he was about to take flight.

I tried to reassure Elmo that the slow burn was in his best interest. "Elmo, at your age why not savor love making? Go slow. I think you're putting too much pressure on yourself. And for Pete's sake, get your immunizations."

"Ridiculous," the cantankerous Deidre added.

"Deidre's correct, Max," whispered Dawn. "The quickie suits Elmo. We don't want to pressure Elmo and kill the golden goose."

"Can't argue with you about that," I replied.

❀ ❀ ❀

"We live in a fantasy world, a world of illusion. An excellent task in life is to find reality."

Iris Murdoch

CHAPTER FORTY-EIGHT

"The Far Side Of The Wall"

E xcept for Elmo, living with social distancing and Covid restrictions was becoming difficult if not oppressive. The residents in my condo complex were angry about the closed tennis courts and other amenities.

Even Ms. Jones, an eighty-five-year-old widow whose condo faced mine, was up in arms. I roared when I saw "OPEN THE POOL" emblazoned on a sheet hanging from her patio railing.

Business was slow, too. Emma's Bookstore couldn't rival the Internet. Sandra, my business partner, recommended we curtail our store hours to Wednesday and Saturday. Thanks to Sandra's vigilance, we had enough capital to keep Emma's Bookstore afloat unlike some of Fairden's retail merchants and restaurant owners.

It was my turn to open the store. I drove into town to post the revised store hours and check the mail. As I stepped inside the phone rang.

"Good morning, Matt."

"What's up Elmo?"

"The Feds just announced the border with Mexico was open. I'm flying to Cabo. Do you want to come along?"

Without thinking, I said, "Sure. When are we leaving?"

"Just as soon as I can arrange for the corporate jet."

"A private jet?"

"Use of the jet was a part of my retirement incentive."

"Oops. I just remembered. I need to return by Tuesday night."

"Can do, Matt."

I called Sandra.

"Matt, we need to talk," was all she said.

I knew I was in trouble. "I'll call you from Mexico."

I never called. I knew what to do, but I just didn't do it.

❊　❊　❊

Forty-eight hours later, I was sipping a poolside bloody mary. I enjoy a morning beverage.

Some of the most significant conversations I have over coffee are with myself. Trust me. The voices in my head don't lie.

My respite was short-lived. In the distance I watched the hotel manager and an attendant grapple with a drunk floundering in the lazy river. They succeeded and dumped the poor soul in a dilapidated wheelchair. The old fool waved to the on-lookers.

That was enough excitement. I looked forward to a relaxing day.

Max, Elmo, and the twins are night owls. I was surprised when they showed up at the pool.

"Where's Max?" I asked.

The sisters looked at one another and smiled. "We left him at Cabo Wabo. Boy, can he drink. He's probably sleeping it off."

I shrugged and pointed to the gathering at the pool bar.

"Please excuse us, Daddy. Time for breakfast." The twins scampered to the pool, jumped in, and claimed two bar stools. That's when the fireworks started. Until, the Double D's arrived all eyes were on a tattooed brunette Adonis accompanied by an elderly geezer, I mistook for her grandfather.

"The Pool Bar Incident"

I finished my bloody mary, when all hell broke out at the pool bar. I casually walked toward the the bar pretending not to be curious. Holy smokes! The geezer appeared to be in distress. He gasped, grabbed his chest and slid beneath the surface.

Deidre frantically waved and shouted for Elmo to get help. In desperation, Deidre took a deep breath and submerged. Remembering her Girl Scout training, Deidre threw a choke hold on the guy. Max, standing poolside pushed his way through the croud and grabbed a hank of the drowning guy's hair and - kaboom! - he tore off the guy's glued toupee. The old man popped to the surface and screamed.

Elmo, fearing for Deidre's safety, jumped into the pool. Elmo couldn't swim. He momentarily flopped around then disappeared. The patrons watched and laughed.

Unbeknownst to the twins and Elmo, the devious old man had pulled this routine before. The lech feigned helplessness. His flailing hands pawed helpless Deidre. He pulled her under. Deidre gave him a swift kick. The despicable jerk gulped water and floated to the surface.

Once again I spotted the pool attendant frantically pushing a wheelchair toward the bar. The wheels wobbled and squealed as it bounced over the pool deck. I rushed to help.

The bartender realized Deidre's quandary and stopped serving drinks.

"Where is Elmo?" shouted Dawn.

Elmo surfaced and gasped for air.

Deidre shouted, "Hey, there's nothing funny about this."

The unruly crowd, intent on a good time, just kept laughing and demanded the bar reopen.

"Come on, Daddy. We are out of here," said Deidre.

Catcalls were the thanks my friends received for their heroic efforts. I'm certain that some of the guests thought the scenario was staged. The front desk received so many encore requests that the manager "comped" Elmo's room for the remainder of the holiday.

❊ ❊ ❊

"Sylvia In Cabo"

The next morning, I decided to skip my morning poolside beverage and walk into town. I needed to preserve my sanity. I invited Max to accompany me. We perused the shops and stopped for a light lunch. A cruise ship was moored offshore and the marina was packed with tourists.

Following our walk, I decided to take a poolside siesta. I found an empty lounge chair and collapsed. I was awakened by a gathering of what appeared to be new arrivals. Then I heard a familiar voice. *It can't be.*

I sat up and spotted a dead ringer for Sylvia, Elmo's estranged wife; all six feet of her. I popped on my floppy hat and sunglasses hoping she would not recognize me.

I lowered my sunglasses and squinted hoping to get a better look. *Oh my gosh! It is Sylvia in that soft pink string bikini. And she looks fabulous.*

Suddenly, Sylvia turned. I glared. Lo and behold, or lower and behold, I discovered Sylvia had a pair of acrobatic humpback whales tattooed on her buttocks. The playful whales maneuvered quite comfortably each time Sylvia took a step.

Sylvia waved and called to the bevy of young companions, "Ladies gather round."

I'd recognized Sylvia's deep-throated voice from years of smoking pot and Regius Double Coronas. Elmo told me that Sylvia smoked weed since her elementary school days and never got addicted. It didn't stunt her growth either. I hesitate before including marijuana in this anecdote. In other words, forget I mentioned it.

Getting back to Sylvia, her companions were a sight for sore eyes. Some sported brightly colored thongs, while others wore beach rompers, an excellent incentive for a drink at the pool.

I put on my sunglasses and looked for another lounge. *Elmo is in for quite a surprise. But I'm not running upstairs with the bad news.*

Holy smokes. Three more companions arrived. One carried a soft guitar case slung over her shoulder. The word "Drool " was embroidered on the case. I recalled Elmo telling me that Sylvia had managed "Drool," a grunge band. I wondered if she was here for a band reunion. That's it! A "Drool" reunion. *Time had been kind to these ladies.*

I ducked, but Sylvia spied me before I could escape.

"Matt Nagle. Elmo told me you were in Cabo. So happy to see you again."

"Thank you, Sylvia. Forgive me, but I thought you were in India."

"I arrived in the States a few weeks ago. Didn't Elmo tell you?"

"No."

"Elmo offered to fly me to Cabo. We have several legal matters that need to be resolved. Elmo seems too accommodating. Do you think Elmo wants to dump me, Matt? He's addicted to those trashy Skipper sisters. Nothing but trouble. I've warned him."

"Elmo hasn't revealed his marital plans to me, Sylvia. And I don't offer advice about his relationship with Dawn and Deidre."

"Well, the more those two spend, the less there is for me," Sylvia protested.

"Excuse me for asking, but who are those ladies?"

"These are the survivors of a garage band I organized.

When the girls heard, I was headed to Cabo, they decided to join me. This is a beautiful resort and very romantic, too."

I caught the gleam in Sylvia's eyes. Sylvia pointed to the high-rise building.

"I'm staying in the penthouse suite. Feel free to drop by Matt. These ladies enjoy a good time. One proviso: wear a Speedo."

That was the last time I saw Sylvia.

* * *

"Verrry Interesting. But Stupid!"
Artie Johnson

CHAPTER FORTY-NINE

"Will The Good Times Ever Return?"

Odd, but since returning from Mexico, I don't see Elmo and the twins as often as before. I called Max and invited him for breakfast.

"I finished your manuscript, Max. However, there are several details you need to review. You may have inadvertently included too many politically correct remarks."

"I'll take a raincheck, Matt. Let's wait a week or two."

Inexplicably, Max's priorities appeared to have changed. I didn't pressure him for an explanation. I suspected something big was on the horizon.

As for Elmo, Sandra heard that Elmo franchised several Jugz locations. He appointed a new CEO for Jugzjava.com. Rumor has it that Elmo is getting back into the music business.

Covid and its variants are still with us. There's a lot of confusion. The federal Covid-19 declaration has ended. In otherwords, "treatment is about to become more expensive for individual Americans." But the experts say it isn't over. I don't know how the experts can tell. Max mentions Covid approximately sixty times in his memoir. He thinks Covid is here to stay. I guess we'll have to adapt.

✻ ✻ ✻

Earlier, Max referred to the downside to living in a so-called niche retirement community. When people surround themselves with like-minded individuals, the residents tend to be isolated from varying points of view. In some ways this may be happening to Fairden.

The Great River Gazette has been sold to a media giant known for liquidating a company's assets, and going digital. That seems to be a nationwide trend. Local news is covered at a distance. Retired couch potatoes are glued to their tribal, I meant to say "favorite," TV station noshing chips. Hopefully not Cheetos. Cheetos fans have a nasty habit of sucking Cheeto dust or "Cheetle" off their fingers. Cheetle, the popular name for the dust, stains clothes and it's a dead giveaway if you're having an affair or stepping outside the box.

* * *

Emma's Bookstore is busy. Sandra and I have "new normal" store hours. The lockdowns are gone, and the quarantines are voluntary. I have a Covid flashback when I spot a shopper wearing a surgical mask.

Lately, I have a tendency to recall the years in relationship to "before and after" the pandemic; my mental timeline. Hopefully, I made the most of the years in between.

So, what is the new normal? I'm not sure, but I have some trepidation as I approach the portal.

"Matt, I dreamt the new normal will be a cruel and unforgiving beast."

Dawn's revelation caught me off guard. "I don't know. But it's time to move to the bright side of the road," I told her. Perhaps I'm being to hopeful about the future.

* * *

Bookstores and Polarization

Sandra's unique marketing skills have kept Emma's Bookstore afloat. We did have a tiff over our book display. Sandra suggested we divide the two display windows into red and blue. We didn't. I insisted we balance our inventory, red, blue, and purple.And that's a task.

So far our sales are about fifty-two percent blue with 48 percent red and purple according to Sandra's account. How Sandra came up with that ranking is beyond me. But, I don't want another tiff.

One thing I know for sure: the public lacks tolerance for opposing points of view.

Sandra's banned books marketing ploy proved successful. We rented a lockable glass book display. The display limited us to the top fifty of the more than 1,600 books banned from schools and libraries. What could we do, but ban the remaining 1,550. At the end of the day, the locked display did raise our customers' curiosities according to our part-time clerk with the display case key.

Since Emma's Bookstore joined the Internet, our sales are soaring. Sadly, my novels are on the back shelf. Mushy romance, followed by crime and thrillers, are the best selling genres in Emma's catalog.

"When it comes to a book, I want emotional satisfaction; an illicit one-nighter or a hero providing justice when the system fails," Elmo insisted.

"I see where you're coming from," said Max. "Dismal times demand lighthearted, righteous, 'feel-good' endings."

"That leaves you out, Matt," said Max. Elmo agreed.

"Do you have to be so truthful?" I asked.

"My friend, in today's crazy world, narrative outlives truth," Elmo replied. "I'm being honest with you. Leave truth out of it. People accept facts as true if the facts agree with what they beleive."

Max and I looked at one another and shrugged. "Elmo, that's profound," I remarked.

"Stop smirking, Matt. This country isn't out of the woods, yet," Elmo protested. "My stocks took a dump. I must keep a closer eye on the market rather than the twins."

"I'm tired of being scared, Daddy," Dawn whimpered.

"Me, too," Deidre agreed. "I get pleasure from a thriller or murder mystery. But I'm feeling angst about the road ahead. And that makes me shiver."

"Did you hear that Matt? Deidre's anxious and she has bare-bones animal instincts," said Elmo.

Max nodded in agreement. "Maybe Deidre has a handle on the new normal."

Elmo said, "The new normal is here. We better get used to it. That goes for you too, Matt. Readers want a happy ending."

❄ ❄ ❄

"Everyone appreciates your honesty,
until you're honest with them.
Then you're an asshole."
            George Carlin

CHAPTER FIFTY

"A Takeaway"

Enter Matt Nagle.

W hen I began editing Max's faux memoir I knew nothing about organizing a garage band. I'm still clueless. I feel that making music is like a harmonious marriage. It requires humility, patience, and compromise.

I did learn the difference between a solo performance and playing with a band. The biggest intangible is ego. Trying to organize your group into a balanced sound is a challenge.

"Matt, convincing a garage band to arrive at a degree of co-operation can be a near impossibility. When we first discussed my memoir, you thought a garage band would be fun. The task sounds more like a marriage, right? Now you know why bands and marriages don't last."

"Frankly Max, I found band break ups are difficult to track since many members form new bands, while others reconnect for a reunion tour. And the divorce rate for the sixty-five and older crowd has more than tripled. Roughly, six percent of divorced couples marry each other again."

"Matt, please spare the research."

"I also read that bands split over sex, drugs and jealousy."

"Ah, I find that a little far-fetched for a garage band. On the other hand, it sounds intriguing," Max replied with a smile. "Selecting musicians to match my personality is like finding the perfect partner. I have a low pain threshhold." Max frowned.

"I'm clueless about marriage, too, Max. It's like looking through the wrong end of the honeymoon telescope. A telescope helps to see thing clearly. But looking through the wrong end makes them less clear and further away. I know now that lucky couples married a spouse who tolerates their nonsense."

"Does that include writers and musicians, Matt?"

"Not when it comes to their idiosyncrasies. Hemingway made it clear. 'When you stop doing things for fun you might as wll be dead.'"

* * *

"Often the hardest songs to play well are the simple ones with just a few chords."

Marty Jourard

* * *

Anyway let's get down to business. Here are my takeaways from Max's faux memoir.

Bands will break up and that can be stressful.

"Your right-on, Matt. There's a difference between a tiff and a riff." Max said. "Of the top ten life stressors, I'd rate a band break up between a job loss and getting married. Here's my advice. Consider your age, your health, and your emotional state before starting a garage band. Living the life of an aging rocker or record producer can have a disastrous impact."

✳ ✳ ✳

Think twice before you remarry your ex-wife. Do you need the stress?

As the song goes: "The good life lets you hide all the sadness you feel."

All tolled, the words, loneliness, unhappiness, and complicated appear more than eighty times in Max's memoir. It took courage for Max to reveal his feelings. And that can be painful.

Americans are searching for happier times. When I listen to Tony Bennett sing "The Good Life," my mind wanders back to a simpler place in time.

"Hold on, Matt. Is that true? You fabricated the good times; the corny poetic bullshit in my memoir," Max protested.

"Granted, I embellished a few passages. Verisimilitude adds an appearance of reality to your memoir. Isn't that what you asked me to do right from the giddyup?"

"Matt, are you saying my memoir is a novel?"

"Max, all novels are fiction, but not all fiction is novels. You're the one who wanted to add different perspectives."

"Isn't that woke?"

"Max, everyone seems to have their own definition of woke, just as long as it fits their argument. All it accomplishes is starting an argument. Woke is so overused, it has lost it meaning. It's becoming musty. Calling someone 'woke' amounts to demanding they shut up."

"Matt, you make it sound like freedom of speech only extends to people who appear to agree with your side?"

"You may be right. Albeit, I'm not saying 'I'm okay, but you are sick and twisted.'"

"Come to think of it, are people intentionally promoting

these polarizing controversies?"

"Yes, I believe there are individuals making big bucks by spreading fear. Politics is burning bridges between families and friends."

"Matt, some folks don't give a shit. At the end of the day, they pour a snifter of Henri IV Cognac and relax."

"Not quite, Max," I replied. "Experts claim the best way to drink Cognac is from a 'tulip' glass," I said with a smile."

"There you go again, Matt, with you research."

❊ ❊ ❊

"The one heresy that no tribe seems to allow is a refusal to hate the other tribe."

Russel Moore.

CHAPTER FIFTY-ONE

"We Had It All."

Enter Matt Nagle. I met Elmo French at Jugz the other night. He told me that Sylvia returned to India. Just between us, it's rumored that Sylvia's guru is a figment of her imagination.

She lives alone in an apartment near Mumbai's famous Bollywood Movie Studios. Elmo said Sylvia had a bit part in Bollywood's recent film, The Three Idiots.

Remember Dawn? How could you forget flirtatious Dawn? She constantly nagged Max about life in the funeral home and stuffing mice. Bless her creative heart. According to Elmo, Dawn recently received an award for her Christmas mouse displays. I'll bet that you'll see mice decorating Saks Fifth Avenue's windows next Christmas.

And determined Deidre is a phlebotomist at the VA hospital. She earned a reputation as a patient advocate.

The Skipper sisters are an important part of Max's memoir.

Elmo is still searching for love. Confidentially, he keeps a sleeping bag behind the couch of a wealthy lady friend over at Springwater Senior Living.

Elmo's big news - "I'm selling Jugz to a retired hedge fund portfolio manager. Time for me to let go and spend time on something that grabs my fervor. I've invested in a recording studio across the river in Millcreek."

Elmo met Ann Trotter, a while back. She was in town visiting friends. Max and Ann never divorced. They reached an understanding.

Elmo said, "Ann was blunt. Divorce is too complicated." I agree. One thing leads to another.

239

Speaking of complicated, Elmo and Max live in a very complex world. They can be sad and happy simultaneously and never ever recognize it.

I asked Elmo,"Do you think something is missing in your life?"

"I'm not sure. I guess that's just my personality. I know I'm a character. I enjoy my eccentricities. Frankly Matt, I miss our conversations at Jugz."

"And how is Max?" I asked.

Elmo shrugged. "Haven't heard from him. Max talked about selling his condo and buying a small motor home." Elmo nervously shuffled and scratched his head. "Max told me that he lost track of what really mattered in his life."

"And what's that?" I asked.

"The simple things," Elmo said.

"I don't get it," I responded. "How did things get so complicated? The word 'happy' appears dozens of times in Max's faux memoir. It's such a simple word."

"Max told me that he envied my wealth, the twins, and most of all my 1953 Buick. I guess one thing does lead to another. Suddenly we're chasing 'stuff' that makes life even more complicated."

Surprisingly, the wrinkles between Elmo's eyebrows deepened, and his shoulders drooped.

"We lost touch," Elmo confessed. "At first I felt blindsided. Now, I'm thankful for the good times. He turned away to blot his tears. "Max could move a million miles away, and that wouldn't ruin our friendship."

Tears glistened on Elmo's cheeks. "And I screwed up," he said.

"How?" I asked.

Elmo paused for a moment to wipe away the tears.

"I didn't take time to listen to my friend. Instead, I went into my usual rant about how hard I worked to get the things Max desired. I'm so sorry."

I didn't respond. For some reason I felt uncomfortable. I

glanced at my watch to signal I had to leave.

"Matt, I know you are in a hurry. Before you go please tell me, what happened to Max's faux memoir?"

"I finished the manuscript. Max never met with me for the final edits. I embellished some scenes and fabricated others; it's one hell of an oxymoron. Nevertheless, I'm leaving it up to Max to complete the final edit and remove anything that smells of political correctness."

❋ ❋ ❋

It's time to close my story about Max Trotter's memoir and the fantastic four's saga. The next time you visit Fairden, please stop by Emma's Bookstore. Perhaps one day you may discover *The Politically Incorrect Max Trotter* displayed on an endcap. You'll have to excuse me. My 16-ounce Teaser, with whipped cream, is ready. I must skedaddle .

After sharing Max Trotter's story I admit that we had it all!

❋ ❋ ❋

"There was truth and there was untruth, and if you clung to the truth even against the whole world, you were not mad."

George Orwell, 1984

ROGER QUINN JR

AFTERWORD

Thank you for reading *The Politically Incorrect* Max *Trotter*.

Cultures create words to express what is valued. Americans have become obsessed with words in the form of political correctness. In the Prologue, Matt Nagle cautioned readers that some might find Max's memoir offensive while others might my discover some excellent stuff.

It was my intention to share the story of a septuagenarian in fear of losing his self-worth in a culture that glorifies youth, wealth, and power.

The tale of our fearless foursome – Max, Elmo, Dawn, and Deidre – is a faux memoir. It's fabricated, embellished... a pack of lies."

I recall Elmo French saying, "Leave truth out of it. People accept facts as true if the facts agree with what they believe. Nevertheless, there is an underlying truth to the concocted story: People have lost their sense of humor.

Columnist Pamela Paul writes, "Political correctness used to be funny. Now it's no joke."

Why make life more complicated than it is?

I don't know the answer. I intended to tell Max's story. Then Elmo, Dawn, and Deidre appeared, each with their longing for self-fulfillment, the long journey from what they were to who they had become.

While funeral home life may appear stifling for Max, it provided ample time to practice his piano and learn taxidermy. Today, rock 'n roll invigorates his life.

The erstwhile bon vivant, Elmo French, owned three cars. Today, he owns one car, a 1953 Buick, and lives a modest lifestyle. Elmo recently opened a not-for-profit recording studio. He derives pleasure seated at a massive analog soundboard recording amazing garage bands.

Ironically, the Skipper sisters turned out to be unlikely heroines. The term heroine hasn't fallen out of style yet. It just isn't used a lot. The Skippers neither sought nor received sympathy for their behavior or circumstances. They are survivors in a materialistic world. Real heroines, and heroes, don't need superpowers. Author Maya Phillips, reminds us: "We need humans - being good, being bad. Humans make mistakes. They fail and still try to stay honest in a broken world."

After editing Max's faux memoir, I've learned my lesson, too. Readers want a happy ending.

RIVER RISING

An Excerpt From Roger Quinn's Forthcoming
Novel, *RIVER RISING.*

It was a humid moonless evening when Marilyn
Nadel rendezvoused with Eric Norman at the Deepmarsh
Community Spa. Hours earlier, Marilyn's husband flew to
Japan for a ten-day business conference. The mischievous
Marilyn sported the body of an eighteen year old. Eric
Norman, fourteen years her junior, is the most recent
addition to the Nadel's guest list and tonight's companion for
what Marilyn called a "spa soiree."

The Homeowners Association installed updated
surveillance cameras following a hot tub tragedy. The
circumstances are unclear, but probably the husband, 70, and
the wife, 65, were having sex. The investigation concluded
that the wife suffered a heart attack and collapsed on her
husband. An attendant discovered the couple called 911, but
it was too late. Few homeowners now use the hot tub in the
evening.

Nevertheless, Marilyn relished the risk. Eric, no altar
boy but uninitiated to the joy of sex with an older woman of
Marilyn's ferocity, had no idea the surprise awaiting.

A lamp post illuminated the spa enough for the security
cameras, but Marilyn came prepared. The capricious Marilyn
stepped back into the shadows and approached the camera
from behind; she quickly stepped around and misted the
camera lens with wasp spray.

"All clear," she whispered to Eric. Marilyn kicked off her heels and slipped out of her cover-up. "Come-on. Don't be bashful," she urged Eric. And with that, an impetuous, Marilyn grabbed Eric's pant waist and said, "Let's go, big guy."

Unbeknownst to Marilyn, a distant pool camera captured their seasoned foreplay.

"Damn. This tub cover is heavy," said Eric.

"I'll help," said Marilyn. "Together now lift," she ordered.

Suddenly, Eric screamed, "Holy shit!" As they raised the heavy cover, a pale gray body floated to the surface.

❊ ❊ ❊

Other Books By Roger Quinn

THE TRINITY CONSPIRACY. Hunt war criminals at work in the U.S. Reveal the bargain made to secure Nazi "scientific research" to put a man on the moon.

THE INNOCENT ASSETS CONSPIRACY. Discover the connection between the government's covert mind control project, a sunken German U-boat, and a series of murders that spell disaster for US President, Katherine Grace Stone.

TURN YOUR LIFE INTO A NOVEL: A Motivational Guide To Establishing A Writing Routine.

The Deepmarsh Mystery Series

GREED, A Short-Term Rental Nightmare. A greedy, creeping invasion of an international rental corporation threatens Deepmarsh Village, a retirement community near Fairden, South Carolina. The creative plot is slow to build, which only enhances the anticipation and surprise readers will feel as the book comes to an end.

DEEP DECEPTION. A chemical plume threatens the region's freshwater source, undetectable by taste, appearance or odor. *DEEP DECEPTION* is a character-driven novel where each protagonist is provided with a thoughtful and detailed background that allows the reader to create connections with the characters.

BOOK CLUB DISCUSSION

The Politically Incorrect Max Trotter is a good-natured tale. Max Trotter is more self-effacing than not. Nevertheless writers walk a fine line in honing their craft with an ever-expanding list of cancel culture taboos that reflect today's cultural divide garnished with despair and loneliness.

1. Can one be a novelist and manage their reputation at the same time?

2. Words are powerful. How do they divide?

3. The Illusions of Truth. When heard over and over again, it makes no difference if statements are true or false.

4. Perception becomes reality. At a time when our nation needs unity, those who call themselves leaders win popularity by inspiring contempt and arousing suspicion.

5. At what point in life does one discover the difference between forgetting where you tossed your car keys and not knowing what the keys are for?

6. **Do older men fear losing their self-worth in a** culture that glorifies, youth, wealth, and controversy?

Bits and pieces from the news media:

7. An overwhelming parallax: locations look different when viewed at unique angles.

8. "We've been doing this for so long that people don't think there's any other way."

9."Every person must choose how much truth they can stand."

* * *

www.ingramcontent.com/pod-product-compliance
Lightning Source LLC
Chambersburg PA
CBHW020746250626
47155CB00003B/944